KINSER HILL

A TENNESSEE FAMILY TRIUMPHS OVER ADVERSITY

JULIE KINSER
HUFFMAN

ISBN:978-1-7346637-0-9

Edited by Ava Coibion
Book Cover Design by Tanja Prokop at Book Cover World
Book Interior Design by Andrea Reider

This book is dedicated to my father,

Wesley Luther Kinser, III,
(December 21,1932—
March 18,1996)

and to my mother,
Carol Ann Tidwell Kinser Thomason.

I could not have been blessed with better parents.

Introduction

Imagine my surprise when I learned about the deeply troublesome past in my family history. I grew up believing that my family was typical, and perceived us as being very similar to the other families living nearby. I was completely unaware of the skeletons in the family closet, and of the deep heartache and legal trouble on my father's side of my family. My ancestors residing on Kinser Hill in Athens, Tennessee, were the recipients of shocking and damaging news many times over the course of their lives. And though they may have kept certain details to themselves, the consequences of personal tragedy spilled over into the lives of future generations.

As a result of my research, my distant relatives are no longer just names to me. Writing this book has brought these lovely people to life, and I have experienced both joy and pain as I have considered the lives they lived. I have teared up as I imagined the dark and agonizing emotions inside of them as they persevered through their devastating experiences. As I studied the various photos, letters, poems, and newspaper articles that were saved and collected in the past, I was able to piece together a chronological story of their lives. As I have written my story about them, these relatives have come alive.

I've always been curious about the lives of my family on Kinser Hill, but it wasn't until recently that I began my own serious research and investigation. What I discovered amazed me.

My grandmother and mother had told me interesting details of the extraordinary events of my family. Oh how I wish that I'd been more curious in my younger years and asked my relatives questions—to think that I could have acquired so many more facts in the way of my family history does instill some regret. I do remember the shock I experienced upon hearing about the tragic demise of my great grandfather and the foolish acts that brought legal trouble for my grandfather.

I am not really sure how I ended up with my grandmother's newlywed photo album in my possession, but I can only say WOW to describe it—it is truly such a treasure trove. There were many details of her younger life that I never knew happened. Certainly, many of these recent discoveries had been stuck in a closet or drawer and untouched for possibly decades. A few years ago my cousin sent me the scrapbook that our great aunt, Marie Kinser, had made when she was in high school and that too was a gem. As I read through the pages in the scrapbook, looked at photos and compared times and dates, I discovered how much adversity my great grandmother and her children had endured, as well as the personal troubles my grandmother and my father encountered. I concluded that this was a story that needed to be told and passed on to future generations. I wanted my children and future bloodline to appreciate the triumph over adversity that my father and his sister were able to achieve, and the life they were able to create for themselves as a result.

In September 2019, my son, Stefan and I travelled to Athens, Tennessee, for my continued family research project. We walked the land where Kinser Hill once existed. We visited the local museum and viewed photos and items relating to my family history. Members of the Athens Historical Society were ready with documents, maps, and helpful suggestions for completing this project.

The house on Kinser Hill has been torn down. The school located right down the hill, Tennessee Wesleyan University, bought the land years ago and built a baseball field and sports facility on the top of that hill. I can't think of a better new beginning for a place like Kinser Hill, one that put behind many sorrows and set the stage for a new purpose to be found. Kinser Hill is a place from the past: but it is a place that is not forgotten.

Acknowledgements

Thanks to my mother, Carol Ann, and my sisters, Amy and Lee Ann, who provided photos, newspaper articles and moral support.

Thanks to my cousins, Russ and Randall, who sent me family photos and shared memories.

Thanks to my children, Viktoria, Lindsay, and Stefan, who listened attentively to me as I shared new discoveries about my family member's lives.

Thanks to Patsy Duckworth from the McMinn County Historical Society, who provided important details that she had accidentally uncovered reading microfilm at the library. She took a special interest in my book for which I am very grateful.

Thanks to Fred Underdown, President of the McMinn County Historical Society and other members, who were eager to look through historical documents that included information about my family.

Thanks to the McMinn County Living Heritage Museum staff, who searched their archived items to find photos and family artifacts that have formerly been displayed in the museum.

Thanks to Angie Jacobs, who spent a day reading my book with me and giving me input and encouragement.

Table of Contents

"To forget one's ancestors is to be a brook without a source, a tree without a root."

- Chinese proverb

The Unimaginable

It was Monday, on the first of May, in the year of 1922, when Wesley Luther Kinser, Sr. got up early for the busy day ahead of him. He had to get himself to the McMinn County Courthouse, where he was the lead attorney currently working on an important case—there was much more investigation to be done before the deadline, which was coming up in a few short weeks.

McMinn County Courthouse

He swallowed his last sip of coffee and kissed his wife Vesta goodbye. "I'll be home for lunch today, but it will have to be a quick one. I've got a lot on the agenda," he said as he got up to leave for work. Wesley valued their lunchtimes when the children were at work and school and they could get at least a solid thirty minutes alone, but lately he was lucky to have enough time to run across the street to purchase a lunch. "I'll have something ready for you to eat when you get here," Vesta replied.

Before leaving, Wesley ran upstairs to peek in on his youngest child, Wesley Luther Kinser, Jr., who was nicknamed WL. WL was just waking up for school. "Good morning, son," he said softly, pushing the bedroom door ajar.

"Morning, Dad," the sleepy boy replied. He pushed the covers off and sat upright.

"You know, WL, I've been thinking about this upcoming weekend since the moment I woke up. I just can't wait for us to catch a few fish. You have a wonderful day at school, and I'll see you tonight!" WL was turning fourteen in eight days, and the two of them had a fishing trip planned for the weekend.

"Can't wait, Dad!" the boy called after him, as he turned and made his way to the staircase. "Have a great day yourself! See you tonight!" exclaimed WL, his voice high and clear.

Wesley got into his car, which he kept parked in the garage, and drove down the long, winding driveway, the beautiful home receding in his rearview mirror. Everyone in Athens was familiar with the alabaster colored house with the tall, gabled roof perched on the hill, known as Kinser Hill. The Kinsers had lived in the home for decades and were dynamic citizens in the community. Their participation in school and church fundraisers was applauded and Wesley was a charitable man who willingly offered his legal services free of charge to the poor.

Kinser Hill
16 Kinser Place
Athens, Tennessee

Life was good on Kinser Hill. It was a beautiful spring day and Wesley imagined Vesta was spending her morning working in the garden, which was small but nonetheless produced a solid harvest. His wife had been busy planting seedling vegetables for the upcoming summer. The lush and elegant property was something Wesley felt perpetually grateful for. They lived on sixteen acres of land on a beautiful rolling hillside. The home itself overlooked the city and the nearby college. Tall trees surrounded the structure, and the wraparound porch allowed for spectacular views. At this particular time of year, quite possibly his favorite, the foliage was budding and blooming.

Wesley held a steady job with a good income that allowed them to live comfortably in their large two-story Victorian home. It truly was such a beautiful setting to enjoy life and raise a family. Six family members resided in the home, which was filled with loving kindness and support for everyone's endeavors.

At lunchtime, Wesley and Vesta enjoyed a nice meal together as they discussed the upcoming birthday celebration for WL. "It's set, then," said Wesley. "We'll plan to leave early on Saturday morning and drive to our favorite location." "Where you normally fish?" asked his wife. "That's the one. Same old spot, new story. There's nothing like the thrill of the catch for that boy," he said and they both laughed out loud. "He certainly has a zest for it," Vesta sighed.

Fishing was WL's favorite hobby. A father-and-son fishing trip included camping and cooking a fish dinner by the fire. On a clear night, they would look at the stars and identify the constellations. Their favorite spot was perfect for everything they wanted to do. The father and son time was cherished and there was great anticipation for the both of them.

"How can I help? What supplies can I gather for your trip?" asked Vesta.

"Just the food items you've rounded up for us for our past trips. Our camping gear is ready to go. Thank you darling," Wesley replied.

Upon finishing the quick lunch, Wesley bent forward to kiss Vesta goodbye. "Work is waiting on me!" he chuckled. "I'll see you this evening, but it might be a late one for me," he said. "Oh, and by the way, I spoke with Cooper today about paying me for the timber. I'm stopping by this afternoon to get the money he owes us. We agreed on $15.00."

"That's great! I'll keep dinner warm for you," Vesta replied, blowing him a kiss goodbye as he headed for the door. He blew a kiss back, as was a common practice for the two of them, then he walked out of the house to get back to work.

Vesta cleared the table of the lunch dishes and cleaned up the kitchen as she thought ahead for the dinner menu. After some minor dinner preparations, she sat down and started writing a list of groceries and supplies to buy for the camping trip. She was the type of person who planned in advance and she wanted to be sure she had time to get everything in order. This was her baby's fourteenth birthday and she wanted it to be special for him in every way.

About an hour later, Vesta was startled by a knock. She could see through the window that it was a policeman, so she answered the door.

"Hello officer. How can I help you?"

The officer had a very serious look on his face. "Mrs. Kinser, we need you to come down to the police station."

"Why? What is wrong, Officer?"

"Your husband has been shot."

"Is he alright?" she asked, the panic rising in her voice.

"I'm so very sorry ma'am, but he has passed away. We need you to come down to the station so we can explain to you the details of the incident."

Vesta fell to her knees in disbelief, put her face in her hands and began sobbing. The kind officer put his hand on her shoulder and said, "I am so sorry, Mrs. Kinser. This is a very unfortunate situation and your statement is important for the ongoing investigation of your husband's death. This appears to be a homicide, so we will need to collect any details or knowledge you have of the suspect."

"My husband had no enemies. I don't understand why anyone would want to shoot him." Vesta's words came out in gasps.

"I'm so sorry this is required of you at this moment, but it shouldn't take too long. I'll drive you to the station then bring you back home afterwards." The officer helped her to her feet, and she walked out to his police car.

At the police station the details were explained to Vesta. Everything felt unreal. How could it be that her kind and gentle husband could be killed so heartlessly? As she listened to the detective's account of the alleged circumstances of the shooting, she could not believe that what they were describing had been the final moments of Wesley's life. She knew by reputation that the murderer was greedy and self-serving, but hearing that he shot Wesley multiple times and at short range was incomprehensible. She could not fathom that any man could be so evil, especially towards her dear Wesley.

Vesta listened carefully to her legal options but needed time to grieve with her family. To prosecute for first degree murder was definitively her choice and plan, without a doubt. She would not let this criminal get away with his crime—justice would be served for her loving husband and best friend in life. She finished up at the station, overcome with sorrow and exhaustion. The officer drove her home. As she struggled to accept her new reality, she repeatedly asked herself the question...how could this wicked man murder such a kind and wonderful family man?

She turned her thoughts to her children and the horrific news that she would have to bring them. Their lives as a family had been turned upside down. WL was home from school by now and would be the first to hear about what had happened to his father. Her heart sunk at the thought. She needed to call Stuart and Marie at work and ask them to come home immediately, then break the impossible news to them. Tears streamed down her face as she exited the police car and walked through her front door. She had never felt so lost in her entire life. Today was a day that she could have never imagined.

Wesley Luther Kinser was sixty-one years old when he was murdered. Surviving was his wife Vesta Ware Kinser, age fifty-one, his son Stuart Ware Kinser, age twenty-three, his daughter Lila Marie Kinser, age twenty-one, and his son Wesley Luther Kinser, Jr., age thirteen.

Death Certificate of Wesley Kinser—Homicide

The Origin of Kinser Hill

esley Luther Kinser married Vesta Ware on June 10th of 1891. He was thirty years old and she was twenty. Ultimately, Wesley and Vesta enjoyed thirty years of a blessed marriage. They were respected and valued members of the Athens community, who would gladly welcome friends and family into their home.

Wesley and Vesta Kinser

There were few ladies with the fortitude of Vesta Ware Kinser, who was born on Christmas Eve in 1870. After marrying Wesley, she resided on Kinser Hill until passing away on February 21,1964, at ninety-three years old. She was the matriarch of the Kinser family. She made the house a loving home and was a pillar of strength for every member of the family. She endured difficult years along with the deepest of heartaches in her lifetime. Vesta's close friends described her as a Lioness of God—fierce protector of her family, and filled with courage, grace, and unconditional love.

Vesta Kinser photographed with her great granddaughter,
Julie Marie Kinser, in 1960 in her home on Kinser Hill.

Vesta wanted children soon after marrying but it took several years before she could get pregnant. At twenty-six, she became pregnant with her first child. Wesley and Vesta were so excited about the upcoming birth of their baby. They decorated the nursery with lace curtains that Vesta sewed by hand. She used matching fabric for the bassinet. The baby's chest of drawers was full of clothing that were gifts from family and friends. A silver rattle, silver cup, and hairbrush were displayed on a crocheted table covering. A stuffed teddy bear sat atop the dresser awaiting its new best friend. Their baby would receive a royal welcome into a loving family.

Arthur Garland Kinser was born on August 9, 1897. Vesta had noticed that her baby had been quiet and not moving much a few days before he was due. She didn't feel too worried. This was her first baby and she didn't have anything to compare to this birth. When the day arrived to give birth it was a struggle. Sadly, he was not alive when she gave birth to him. Wesley and Vesta were devastated. Along with their families, they mourned the death of Arthur. He was buried at Cedar Grove Cemetery in Athens, Tennessee.

Gravestone of Infant Son, Arthur Garland Kinser

Seven months later, Vesta became pregnant again. She fought with negative emotions, finding it hard to be too enthusiastic with this pregnancy after losing her first child. She was still very much grieving the loss of Arthur but had high hopes for this birth to result in a healthy baby. She would share her fears with her husband and spent time in prayer every day, asking God to watch over her the baby growing inside of her. She was careful to follow doctor's orders.

Vesta gave birth to Stuart Ware Kinser on December 13th of 1898. What a joy to hold that sweet baby boy in her arms! Wesley and Vesta were so grateful to welcome a healthy baby and to be starting their family. More fortune came their way, when a couple years later on August 9th of 1900, a daughter was born to them. They named her Lila Marie and called her Marie. Their family was now complete, with a boy and a girl. Wesley and Vesta enjoyed every minute they spent raising their children. On weekends, Wesley took them fishing and taught them how to farm. Stuart and Marie learned how to grow a garden. Vesta taught Marie to cook, as well as how to complete all kinds of handiwork and needlework. She could sew, knit, and crochet, and felt it was important to pass these skills on to her daughter.

Wesley and Vesta desired to have another child, but years went by and no pregnancy occurred. Vesta was coming to terms with the realization that her childbearing days were over, until one day she discovered she was expecting again. Long since having given up on more children, they were over the moon! What a wonderful surprise it was for Stuart and Marie when they heard the news that their mother was expecting another child! Stuart was nine and Marie was seven, both old enough to anticipate the coming of a new sibling. After seven years of trying to have a baby, their prayers were answered. On May 9th of 1908, Wesley Luther Kinser, Jr., was born. They decided to name him after Wesley, following an age-old tradition of the third son being named after his father.

In 1913, a terrible tragedy struck the family when Vesta's older sister, Mary Plumlee, lost her husband Finis in a deadly car accident. Finis was forty-five years old at his death and Mary was forty-seven. They had not been able to have children together and that had been a source of grief for them. After her husband's death, Mary was distraught and felt very alone. Wesley and Vesta offered her a place in their home, and Mary was grateful to move in with the Kinser family. Stuart was fourteen at the time, and Marie was twelve. Vesta was very busy with the older children's activities, and Mary helped care for WL, as he had not yet started school.

While living with her sister, her heart was able to heal from her loss and overcome her grief. Mary was like a second mother to WL, doting on him as if he were her own child. While Vesta was taking Stuart and Marie to piano, art, and singing lessons, Mary was WL's favorite playmate. They played hide and seek throughout the house and would take the game outside on a pretty day. Nice weather allowed exploring Kinser Hill and a game of kickball. As WL grew older, Mary was a listening ear and gave good advice. Throughout adulthood, WL and Mary maintained a close relationship until she passed away on January 23, 1938. She was seventy-two when she died. Vesta, Marie, and Stuart were deeply saddened by her passing, but WL took the news the hardest. Though he had moved away from Athens, was married and a father, the childhood love he had felt for Mary, and the close bond and relationship they shared had left a lasting impression, and he mourned her death deeply.

The family on Kinser Hill enjoyed many wonderful years together as the three children grew and matured. Due to how their birthdays fell, Stuart and Marie were in the same class at school. Stuart was one of the older students and Marie one of the youngest in the class. They both excelled and were involved in many extracurricular activities. Playing the piano was among their many talents and they often thrilled their family and an audience with their duet. Stuart was very artistic, and painted as a hobby. Marie enjoyed performing in plays and musicals. Like most young girls, Marie kept a scrapbook of childhood memories that could be enjoyed by family and passed on to future generations.

Senior Class Plays
McMinn County High School
ATHENS. TENN.,

AT COLLEGE CHAPEL
Tuesday, May 27, 1919, 8:00 p. m.

Program
DIAMONDS AND HEARTS

Bernice Halstead	Lynn Russell
Amy Halstead	Margaret Elliott
Inez Gray	Marie Kinser
Mrs. Halstead	Elizabeth Erwin
Hannah ("Sis") Barnes	Reva Rankin
Dwight Bradley	Hugh Burns
Dr. Burton	Dillard Francisco
Sammy	Herbert Ray
Abraham ("Bub") Barnes	Lowell Hackler
Attorney	Karl McKeehan
Sheriff	Robert Millard

ENGAGED BY WEDNESDAY

Martin Henry	Lowell Hackler
Arthur Watson	Hugh Burns
Jack	Herbert Ray
Ted	Karl McKeehan
Dick	Robert Millard
Miss Abigail Persons	Grace Moore
Mrs. Watson	Della Erwin
Lucile Persons	Allie Foree
Marie	Themis Hutsell
Jane	Stella Taylor
Mabel	Marie Kinser
Mary	Elizabeth Snyde.
First Girl	Abbie Hutsell
Second Girl	Rossie Torbett
Gypsy	Myrtle Erwin

Marie was in her Senior Class Play.

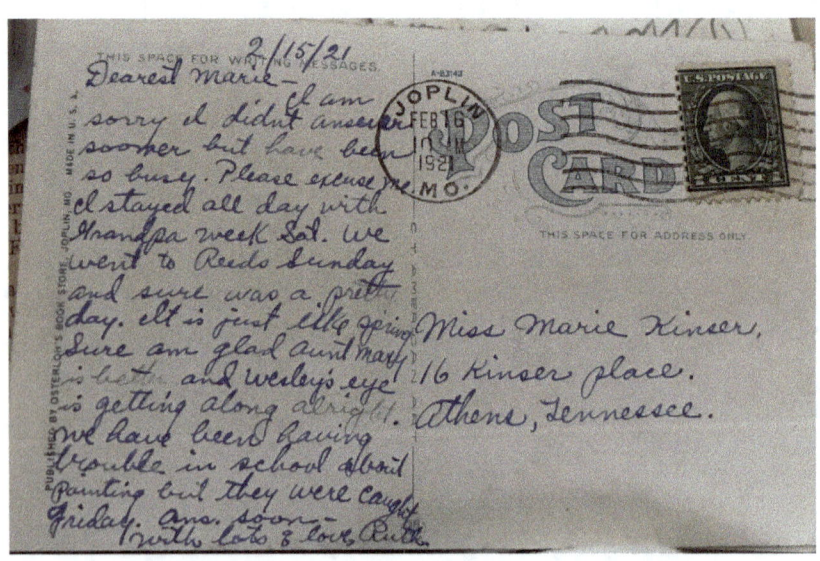

A saved football ticket in Marie's scrapbook.

Marie corresponded with many of her friends and family who lived out of town. She added similar postcards in many pages of her scrapbook.

Reading under a tree and playing with friends were her favorite things to do on Kinser Hill.

Stuart was a very talented artist and Marie cherished
this watercolor he painted for her.

Marie (far left) loved singing and performing.

Misses Grace Oliphant and Gladys Cannon, Prof. A. E. Brown and Mr. J. E. Brown were guests of Miss Marie Kinser Saturday.

Marie loved to entertain on Kinser Hill
and it was published in the newspaper.

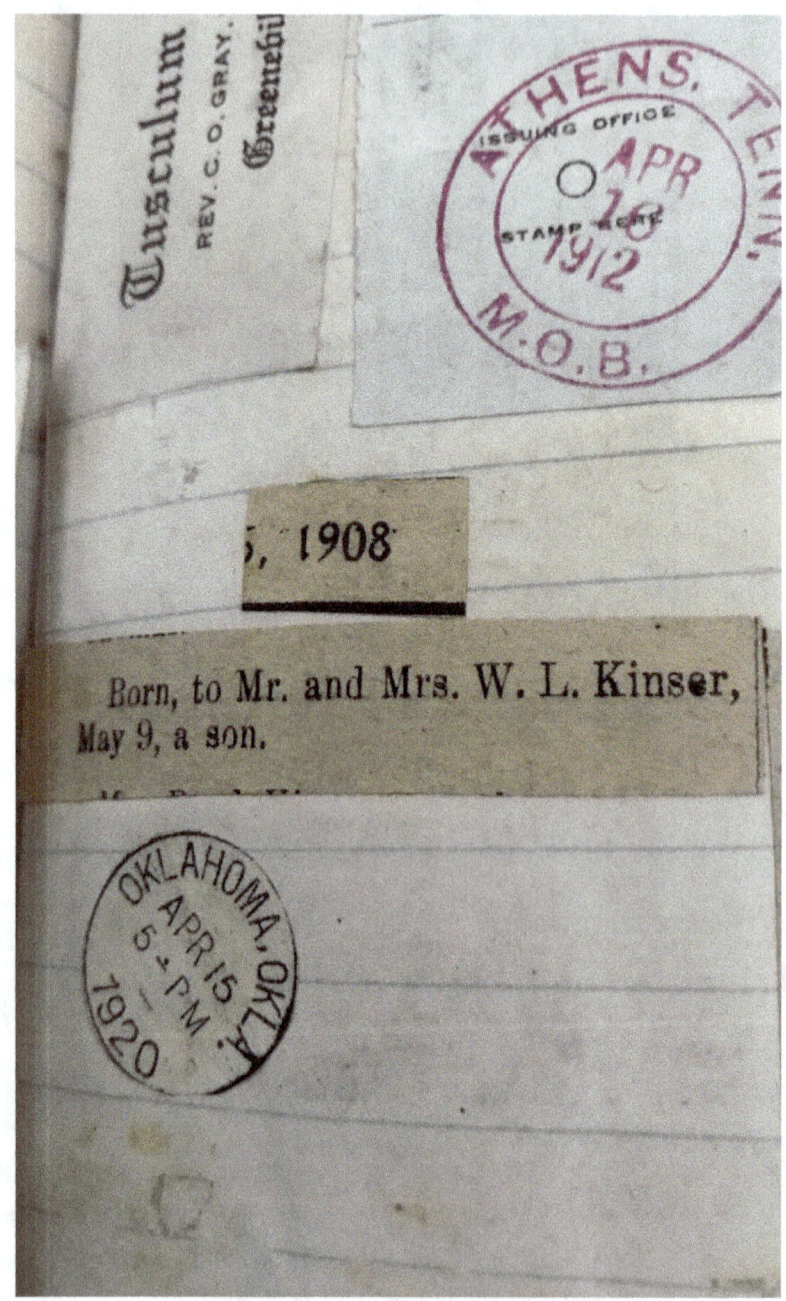

The 1908 newspaper announcement of the birth
of her new brother was added to her scrapbook.

Marie had kept a handmade Christmas card written by ten-year-old Stuart to their father. He had written, "I want to help you all I can." These words were even more cherished after their father's death.

World Famous Tacoma Pear Stockings

Stuart and Marie worked at the local company Athens Hosiery Mill. Stuart worked in shipping and Marie was a secretary. She was proud to have been employed by this company.

Stuart was a man of faith and cherished the Bible his mother gave him.

WL (far right) attended Forest Hill School. Photo was taken in 1915.

A Young Boy's Devastated Life

WL came home from school on May 1st of 1922, to some of the most devastating news a young boy could possibly hear. His father had been murdered. The gun blast to the head was at short range so his father's face was marred and disfigured. For this reason, the authorities advised the family against viewing the body. The morning goodbye he had exchanged with his dad would be the last conversation they would ever have. He would never hear the sound of his dad's voice again.

Vesta was sitting at the kitchen table when WL walked into the room.

"Hello, Mom! How was your day?" he asked happily, but then he noticed the tears in his mom's eyes. It became clear to him that she had been crying for some time, and that something was very wrong. "What's wrong, Mom?"

"Please sit down, WL. I have some very sad news." Vesta took a deep breath and began to tell him about his father. "I am so very sorry to have to be the one to tell you this..."

"What is it, Mom?" WL asked, slowly sinking into the chair across from her, his face filled with trepidation.

"Your father was shot today and he didn't survive. The bullets pierced his heart and instantly killed him."

"What? I don't understand. Are you sure? Are you saying that dad is dead?" The shocking statements had created confusion for him. He was stunned by what he was hearing and didn't believe it was true.

"Yes, the man who shot him has confessed to the shooting, but he is saying that it was self-defense. He is saying that your father became angry, threatened him and tried to fight him. The man said he had no choice but to shoot him because . . . he feared for his life."

"Dad would never do such a thing," yelled WL. Of all people, Vesta knew how deeply WL loved his father, and how fiercely loyal he was to him. The boy broke down in tears. Vesta hugged him, holding him close and doing her best to comfort him. It was a true dilemma for her to know how to comfort a thirteen-year-old boy who had just had his world shattered. They embraced each other and wept. Though she knew that the trauma of seeing his mother weep added to his pain of knowing his father was dead, she could not hold back her tears.

"I need to call Stuart and Marie," she told him. They were at work at the Athens Hosiery Mill that day and rushed home when they received the news about their father. The family spent the rest of the day in shock and disbelief. It seemed impossible that such a travesty could happen to their beloved husband and father.

It was difficult to sleep that night and Vesta laid alone in her bed for the first time in years. Her mind was racing, and she was thinking over the plans for the funeral. She needed to contact their church pastor about the service. She needed to talk to the funeral home staff about the casket and burial. Her mind wandered to thoughts of Wesley's court case that he wouldn't get to complete and how he was looking forward to the fishing trip with WL. She got up and peeked into WL's room to check on him.

As she was opening the door, she caught him closing his eyes, pretending to be asleep. She couldn't blame him if he didn't want to talk to anyone at the moment, not even his mom. She closed the door softly, and walked down the hall to check in on Marie. She was awake. Vesta crawled into bed with her.

"I am so sad. Daddy was the best father a girl could ever hope to have. I have never felt such pain," Marie confided in her mother.

"He loved you with his whole heart, Marie. You were his one and only daughter. He was filled with pride over you. We were very blessed to have him in our lives and will never stop missing him," Vesta said comfortingly.

"The funeral will be in two days. We have time to share our thoughts about your father with the pastor for his eulogy," and they began to discuss the funeral and the future. Both cried together for a while, before exhaustion finally forced them to close their eyes and sleep.

WL laid awake staring at the ceiling, thinking about the fishing trip that he had been looking forward to taking with his dad. His birthday was in one week and it was going to be the saddest birthday, he thought. "How can life continue without my father? I hate that man who killed him, and he will pay for what he has done," he whispered to himself. Then he cried himself to sleep.

That following morning, when he woke up late after a restless night, he could hear unfamiliar voices. He got dressed though had no intention of going to school that day. As he arrived at the bottom of the staircase, to his left were two men from the funeral home sitting in the living room talking with his mother. He could hear them discussing the funeral arrangements. He made a right turn towards the kitchen. He looked for something to eat for breakfast, but it was only because of habit. He didn't feel hungry. He felt empty inside and had an unfamiliar pain in his chest. He didn't fully understand that the ache was because he was brokenhearted. It was still surreal that his father was gone forever. He felt like he was in a bad nightmare, except he knew that there was no waking up from this.

His older brother, Stuart, had walked into the kitchen. "Did you get any sleep last night, WL?" he asked in a voice softer than his usual one.

"Not much," he replied, shrugging.

Stuart gave him a long and silent hug. "I'm going to be there for you," he said. "You are becoming a man, WL, and you need a father figure. I can't replace Dad, but I'll step in anywhere I can." He loved his little brother.

They sat down at the kitchen table and tried to eat some breakfast. They knew it was important to keep up their strength for their mother.

The day after Wesley's death was very tiring for the family. Vesta received phone call after phone call, all having to do with important funeral decisions, and the detectives were asking further questions about the murder suspect. She could hardly think straight, yet it felt like the whole world was demanding that she bottle up her heart and make practical choices about flower arrangements and timelines. News of Wesley's death had spread quickly throughout Athens, so friends and neighbors were dropping off food and expressing their condolences. The grieving family was grateful and gracious, but they were still trying to process, and they had no taste for casseroles or pretty little cakes.

Wesley was laid to rest two days after his death. The funeral service was crowded with family and friends, and the minister from the church delivered a beautiful eulogy. "Wesley was a kind and generous man," the minister affirmed. "He was well-educated and a leader in the community. His work as an attorney benefitted many local citizens. Above all, he was a devoted husband and father." Not only were close friends and family stunned that such a violent act would be carried out against such an outstanding individual, but acquaintances in the whole city of Athens were grieving.

Gravestone in Cedar Grove Cemetery in Athens, Tennessee

WL found it very difficult to listen to the eulogy. He didn't need anyone to tell him that his father was wonderful. He knew that already. He stood by his father's freshly dug grave and held in his anger, his chest feeling as if it would explode. He felt strong hatred towards the murderer, and fantasized of killing him with his bare hands. He wanted that person to suffer the pain exactly as he was suffering. He struggled to hold back the tears produced by his anger. How could such an evil person be allowed to live? he thought. He prayed to God for that awful man's demise. Strike him down and make him suffer, he prayed.

The exhausted family stood in a receiving line to thank people for coming. They politely and gracefully listened to the kind words expressed about Wesley. It became too much for WL. He whispered to his mother, telling her he'd be right back, then he walked down the road where there were no people around him. He just wanted to be alone for a while. He walked in circles, thinking back on the special times he had spent with his dad and how he could talk to him about anything. His dad always had time for him. He would stop whatever he was doing to listen and talk with him if he had a problem. His dad had been his best friend.

The funeral ended and WL walked back to join his mother and siblings. As they walked away they all commented to each other in their own way how hard it was to believe their dad was gone. They all had to adjust their minds to living life without him, and accept that legal proceedings loomed ahead. It would be a trying time for them.

When they arrived at their home, Vesta pulled Stuart aside and told him about the upcoming plans for WL's fourteenth birthday.

"Mother," Stuart responded, gently placing his hand on his mother's forearm. "I will gladly take WL on the fishing trip that Dad planned for his birthday." He walked over to WL who was sitting alone, outside on the porch. The sun was setting, and sunbeams were shining through the trees onto his face. Stuart sat down beside him and together they basked in the warmth of the sun before asking, "WL, would you like me to take you on the fishing trip that you and dad had planned? It seems like too much fun to pass up."

WL looked up at Stuart and stared at him for a moment. Finally, he mustered up a smile said, "That would be great. Thank you." The brothers had something pleasant to look forward to amid the sorrow.

Early on Saturday morning, Stuart and WL prepared to leave for WL's birthday trip. They decided to drive their father's car to the location. They both agreed that it would feel like their dad was with them in spirit if his car was there. They put all the camping gear in the trunk. Vesta packed them their favorite food for camping. She had baked a loaf of bread and cookies.

She packed butter and jam and jars with water so they could make coffee and tea. She hugged her boys goodbye and wished them a wonderful day and night together. "Hope you catch a lot of fish, WL! We're going to have a family celebration for your birthday when you come home tomorrow," she called out as they were driving off.

Stuart and WL set up camp near the riverbank. They fished all day and caught plenty of fish for dinner and breakfast and they had enough to take home to their mother and sister, too. As they cleaned up and arranged the kindling they had collected, the comforting sound of cicadas and frogs vocalizing kept them company. That evening, as they sat by the fire, they looked up at the sky and identified constellations.

"This was dad's favorite part of the camping experience," Stuart said.

"I know," replied WL, his voice filled with affection. "Dad knew so much about astronomy." In the precise moment that WL made that statement, a shooting star flashed across the dark sky. "Wow, did you see that?" he asked.

"Dad heard us talking about him," said Stuart, his eyes glistening.

"And he wanted us to know that he heard us," replied WL.

At that moment, WL recognized that Stuart was not just his brother, but also his best friend. He understood that a memory had just been born, and that more memories were on the horizon, and that not all was lost, so long as he had this bond with his brother.

For the next few years, Stuart and Marie remained at home to provide love and support to their mother and young brother. Dealing with the ups and downs of the murder trial for their father brought great anxiety and stress on the whole family. The family clung to each other, providing love and encouragement.

Who Did It?

A couple of weeks before his murder, Wesley had driven up to Star Mountain to check on his farm property. He was selling some timber harvested from trees growing on his land and he wanted to survey his investment. When he arrived, he saw that more trees had been cut down than had been commissioned. There was a section of trees bordering his neighbor's lot that had been chopped down. As he walked around his acreage, he discovered the obvious problem. George W. Cooper, who owned the neighboring property, had been cutting down trees on his property as well. Hidden behind a hillside, the missing section of trees was not visible from the road. Unless someone walked the entirety of the land, it could easily be missed. Wesley walked upon a bare place on his land where many trees had been cut down. Everything came together—Cooper had been cutting his own trees down on the bordering land in the same area and had crossed over his boundary line and plundered timber from Wesley. Too many trees had been cut to argue that the mistake had been unintentional.

When Wesley arrived home later, he told Vesta about it and said he was going to talk to Cooper. Beforehand, as a precaution, he contacted the logging company that he had hired and questioned them about the timber on his land that bordered Cooper's lot. The contractor confirmed that was not the area where they cut down trees, and that they had been careful to only remove trees in the designated area.

Wesley drove up to Cooper's home and knocked on the door. Cooper answered the door.

"Hello, George, I haven't seen you in a while. How are you doing?"

"I've been really busy tending to farm work. What brings you to my home today, Wesley?"

"I have confirmation that you've been cutting down my trees on my property. It seems you've crossed the boundary line onto my land. You'll need to repay me for my timber," Wesley said.

"I don't have any idea of what you're talking about," Cooper replied flatly, his eyes giving nothing away.

"Cooper, I saw the missing trees on our bordering property. I contacted the company I've hired, and they confirmed that you had been cutting down my trees. Cooper, let's not feud about this. I will have to report this to the police if it continues. If you stop now, I won't report you, but I want compensation for the timber you have cut and sold," Wesley insisted, making it clear that he was serious. He knew that Cooper was aware that he was an attorney, and he hoped that would be on his side in terms of Cooper amicably stepping down. He also knew that he was headed for potential legal trouble, but he stood his ground, waiting for Cooper to respond.

"I don't know what you are talking about," Cooper repeated.

Cooper's stubborn denial didn't change the situation at hand, despite Wesley's realization that this could be an uphill battle. Wesley warned him, "Don't back me in a corner and force me to contact the police, George."

"I'll return next week to check on my land and I'll expect your payment next week." Wesley walked to his car and drove away.

Upon returning home he recounted his conversation with Cooper to Vesta. "I hope he listened to me. I really don't want to report him, but he is a stubborn man."

"Is he having financial trouble?" Vesta asked.

"None that I'm aware of. I would say he just got greedy and thought he could get away with his little caper." The two forgot about it for the next several days, but Wesley was planning to follow up.

On Monday morning, Wesley arrived at his office, but before starting his workday, he picked up the phone, and called Cooper.

"Cooper," he began, "this is Wesley Kinser. I'm at my office at the courthouse today and wanted to ask you to bring by the money you owe me."

"You can come by my place today if you want your money," Cooper barked. "Okay, I'll come by this afternoon. Thanks," replied Wesley. Cooper hung up and prepared himself for the afternoon encounter with Wesley.

After his lunch with Vesta, Wesley drove over to Cooper's farm. When he approached the house, Cooper walked out his front door with a shotgun in his hand. No one will ever know the words exchanged that day between these two men. One thing is for certain, an amicable agreement was not reached because George W. Cooper raised his shotgun and pulled the trigger. Wesley had turned to walk to his car and he was shot in the chest and the head, killing him instantly.

Cooper called the police and reported the incident. He reported that the argument was heated so he shot and killed Wesley in self-defense. The police arrived to find Wesley lying on the ground in a pool of blood. The investigators detailed Cooper's explanation of self-defense. The coroner retrieved

Wesley's body and did their own investigation. Cooper was eventually charged with the homicide.

Over the next two years, there were three trials. The prosecution did their best to convict Cooper of the murder of Wesley. In the first trial, he was convicted of first-degree murder, but it was reversed by a higher court. The second trial was a conviction of second-degree murder, but that too was appealed and reversed. No time in prison was served for the murder. Vesta, Stuart, and Marie attended every trial. After the final day in court, they would go home hopeful but later disappointed and saddened that justice for Wesley was not found. The family felt there was a strong probability of corruption in the legal system, due to the fact that Cooper spent no time incarcerated when evidence spoke to the validity of the crime.

WL missed the court trials because he was in school. He would come home very anxious and eager to hear about how the details and outcome of each trial had played out. He didn't need words of explanation because he could see the distressed looks on his family members' faces. Seeing their hope turn to disappointment and sadness only fueled the growing anger inside of him. The injustice of the murderer walking free when his father died over a frivolous disagreement was beyond his understanding. He wished he could take matters into his own hands.

On November 8, 1924, a verdict of voluntary manslaughter and ten years in the penitentiary was decided upon by the jury in the third trial and it once again was appealed. The pending appeal took time but was to have a verdict within the second week of January 1926. Once again, Vesta and her children had to wait and wonder. The toil of all the trials and the rollercoaster of hope and disappointment wore heavy on all of them. Vesta kept the newspaper articles of the trial results and details.

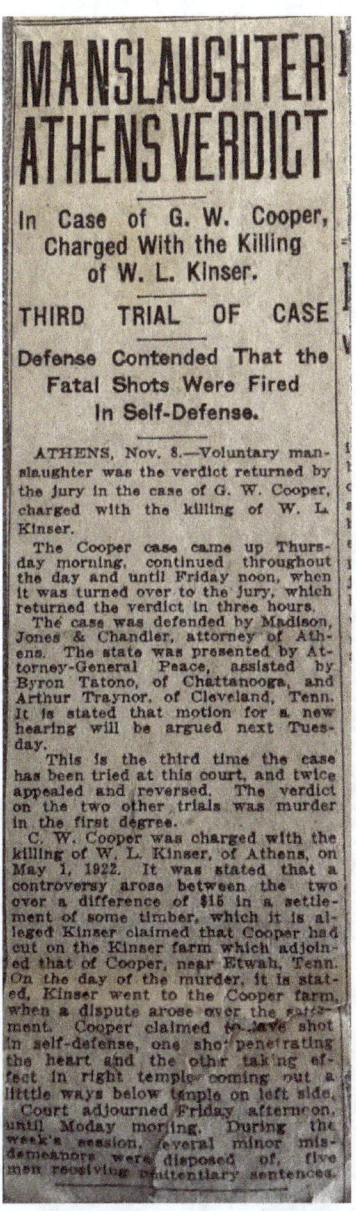

MANSLAUGHTER ATHENS VERDICT

In Case of G. W. Cooper, Charged With the Killing of W. L. Kinser.

THIRD TRIAL OF CASE

Defense Contended That the Fatal Shots Were Fired In Self-Defense.

ATHENS, Nov. 8.—Voluntary manslaughter was the verdict returned by the jury in the case of G. W. Cooper, charged with the killing of W. L. Kinser.

The Cooper case came up Thursday morning, continued throughout the day and until Friday noon, when it was turned over to the jury, which returned the verdict in three hours.

The case was defended by Madison, Jones & Chandler, attorney of Athens. The state was presented by Attorney-General Peace, assisted by Byron Tatono, of Chattanooga, and Arthur Traynor, of Cleveland, Tenn. It is stated that motion for a new hearing will be argued next Tuesday.

This is the third time the case has been tried at this court, and twice appealed and reversed. The verdict on the two other trials was murder in the first degree.

C. W. Cooper was charged with the killing of W. L. Kinser, of Athens, on May 1, 1922. It was stated that a controversy arose between the two over a difference of $15 in a settlement of some timber, which it is alleged Kinser claimed that Cooper had cut on the Kinser farm which adjoined that of Cooper, near Etwah, Tenn. On the day of the murder, it is stated, Kinser went to the Cooper farm, when a dispute arose over the settlement. Cooper claimed to have shot in self-defense, one shot penetrating the heart and the other taking effect in right temple coming out a little ways below temple on left side.

Court adjourned Friday afternoon until Monday morning. During the week's session, several minor misdemeanors were disposed of, five men receiving penitentiary sentences.

1924 Newspaper Clippings of Kinser Murder Trial Results

COOPER CONVICTED OF MANSLAUGHTER

Killed Kinser in 1922—Case Tried Three Times.

Judge Brown Deals Heavy Sentences to Bootleggers and to Burglars.

Chattanooga Times Special.

ATHENS, Tenn., Nov. 8.—The case of George W. Cooper, for the killing of Wesley Kinser on May 1, 1922, was, for the third time since the killing, tried in circuit court here today. This time the jury returned a verdict, after a short session of deliberation, of guilty of manslaughter. The court imposed a sentence of from two to ten years in the state penitentiary. A motion for new trial will be made by the defense.

W. L. Kinser was killed by Cooper on some land belonging to the latter, which was located near Etowah, Tenn. The two men had been in a dispute about a boundary line and the argument became heated to the extent of shooting. Kinser was shot by Cooper with a shotgun three or four times. The plea of self-defense was used by the defendant. Both men were about 60 years old and were property owners in McMinn county.

The November term of circuit court was begun on Monday of this week, but the court adjourned until Wednesday on account of the election. Beginning Wednesday several misdemeanor cases were tried, besides a few which carried penitentiary sen-

As the day of judgement for the future of George Cooper approached, an unexpected event occurred. Cooper was brutally murdered one week before he was to return to court. Originally, it was thought he fell from the hayloft of his barn, and that the fall was intentional, a result of him having committed suicide.

His family informed authorities that he had been very worried and distraught over the upcoming verdict and potential prison time. The second inquest determined that his injuries were not consistent with such a fall. The coroner's report concluded that he had been attacked with a sharp object like an ax or similar tool.

Cooper was found in his barn, severely beaten with the weapon, which resulted in multiple broken bones and injuries to his skull, face and shoulders. Whoever killed him probably knew him—this was certainly a crime of passion. Investigators surmised that the mysterious assailant had hidden in the nearby corn house and waited to ambush him. There was evidence that a person had been sitting in the corner inside the corn crib. There was no robbery and no items were missing from the barn.

Ultimately, George W. Cooper became the victim of his own crime. The murderer was murdered. There was much contemplation in the community over his untimely death. Who else did this man offend? Who was it that despised this man so much that he would hide until the perfect opportunity? Who had such hatred that he would beat this man so badly? It was a tragedy for the Cooper family to lose their husband and father in this way.

But was this an eye-for-an-eye murder? Was this how justice was finally served for Wesley Kinser? Was manslaughter instead of first-degree murder too light of a sentence for Cooper, in the opinion of whoever killed him? So many unanswered questions existed. The assassin was never identified. An investigation of a former police chief named Burkett Ivirs took place and he was considered a suspect in the murder of George Cooper. Ivirs was a good friend of Wesley and was outspoken about the injustice surrounding the trials. No evidence was found to convict Ivirs and the investigation was dropped. There were no more legal proceedings for the Kinser family. This nightmare was finally over.

Stuart and Marie had put their lives and futures on hold to support their mother and brother throughout the years of court trials and WL's upbringing. Three and one half years after their father's death, they were finally released from this ongoing tragedy and injustice fiasco, when they learned that Cooper had been murdered. The Kinser family had to move on from their tragedy, let their hearts heal, and make their way into the future.

Under Sentence
Cooper Murdered

Chattanooga Times Special

ATHENS, Tenn., Jan. 10.—Charged with murder and awaiting t h e decision of the supreme court, George W. Cooper fell, himself, a victim of foul play Saturday afternoon, if the findings of a coroner's jury are correct.

Cooper, who was 59 years old, went from his house, about three miles east of Etowah, to his barn, 200 yards away, to do his chores and was found half an hour later with his skull fractured, his left shoulder broken and his collarbone cracked .

Late Saturday night, a coroner's inquest was held by S. C. Cagle and Will Kelley, but after preliminary examination they were unable to reach a decision and so adjourned until today to collect further evidence.

It was first thought that Cooper had fallen out of the hay mow, but the position of the body proved to be several feet distant from the location of a natural fall, leaving only the alternative of suicide, which was thought impossible by the nature of the injuries.

At this morning's session of the coroner's jury a verdict of death by a sharp instrument was decided upon, because of the broken bones and skull and signs of beating about the face and shoulders. It is thought that an ax or some similar weapon was used by the unknown assailant who killed him.

1926 Newspaper Clipping of the death of George Cooper

Close examination of the barn lot showed tracks from the corn crib running to a small wooded plot which stands a few hundred feet from the barn. Within the crib itself there was a disarrangement of the corn in one corner, which the officers thought might have been used as a hiding place by the criminal.

Cooper was charged with the murder of W. L. Kinser, of Athens, on May 1, 1922. His case has been tried and appealed three times. In the first instance a verdict of first degree murder was returned, only to be reversed by the higher court. At the second trial a second degree verdict was returned and reversed again, while at the third trial he was found guilty of manslaughter and sentenced to ten years in the penitentiary. This is the case which is pending at the present time in which a verdict was expected this week.

The killing of Kinser resulted from a dispute between the two men over a difference concerning timber. Kinser is supposed to have accused Cooper of cutting some trees which stood on the Kinser farm, which adjoins that of the murdered man. On the day of the killing Kinser is said to have gone to the Cooper home in an attempt to collect money for the timber he thought belonged to him.

Cooper maintained in the trials that he killed Kinser in self-defense.

WL Falls in Love

There was a girl at WL's high school whom he became very interested in dating. Her name was Elizabeth Russell. They were in the same class in school. A beauty with auburn hair, she was the daughter of a successful farmer in nearby Calhoun. He was attracted to her not only because of her looks, but also for her character and strengths—she was a motivated student with an outgoing personality. An honor roll student active in 4-H, she was popular among her peers and stood out as a leader. She received awards for her 4-H work and won a trip to Chicago, which was a very big deal for her school and family. Elizabeth had her eye on WL as well, and was reciprocal in her feelings for him. WL and Elizabeth would date on weekends whenever possible, and grew to be crazy about each other.

WL and Elizabeth on a picnic date in the park.

WL and Elizabeth were both contestants for a high school competition. Mutual interests in school activities and subjects drew them closer to each other as friends and companions. They were admired by their fellow students and known as high school sweethearts.

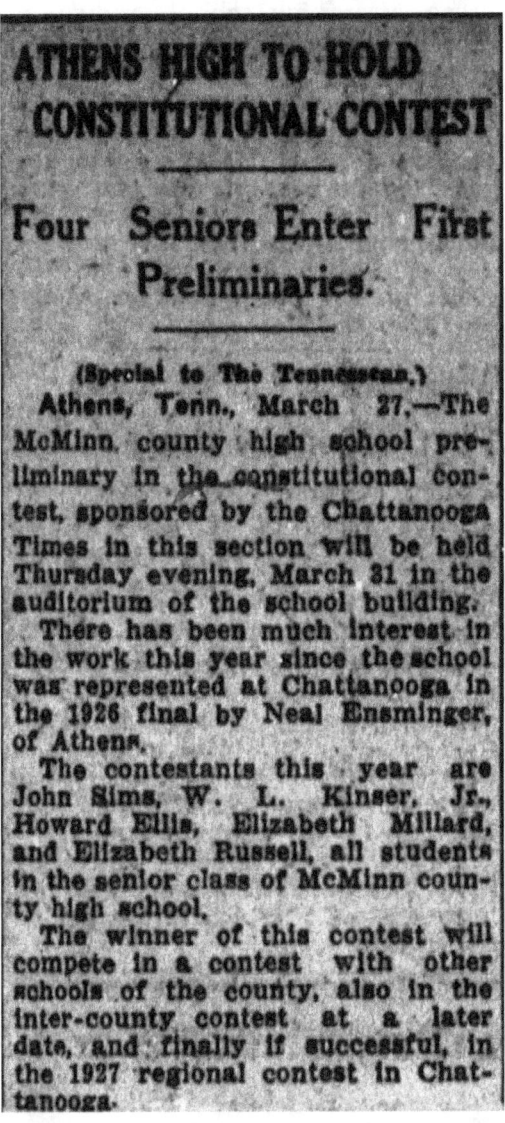

ATHENS HIGH TO HOLD CONSTITUTIONAL CONTEST

Four Seniors Enter First Preliminaries.

(Special to The Tennessean.)

Athens, Tenn., March 27.—The McMinn county high school preliminary in the constitutional contest, sponsored by the Chattanooga Times in this section will be held Thursday evening, March 31 in the auditorium of the school building.

There has been much interest in the work this year since the school was represented at Chattanooga in the 1926 final by Neal Ensminger, of Athens.

The contestants this year are John Sims, W. L. Kinser, Jr., Howard Ellis, Elizabeth Millard, and Elizabeth Russell, all students in the senior class of McMinn county high school.

The winner of this contest will compete in a contest with other schools of the county, also in the inter-county contest at a later date, and finally if successful, in the 1927 regional contest in Chattanooga.

When WL graduated from high school in 1927, he knew he didn't want to stay in Athens. He was ready for new scenery and a fresh start. His life had been turned upside down by the death of his father and the ongoing trials regarding his father's murder had taken a toll on him. He thought a change would be helpful. He enrolled in Tennessee Military Institute in Sweetwater, Tennessee, after high school graduation and started classes in the fall of 1927. Sweetwater was only a thirty-minute drive away.

Elizabeth chose to attend her freshman year at Maryville College in Maryville, Tennessee. They were about an hour drive from each other and though they weren't too far away distance-wise, after a few months, they decided they wanted to go to college together. WL decided to transfer to Maryville. They were thrilled to be together again and see each other every day. When not in class, they were together either studying or talking about their future plans. "I want to marry you and I don't want to wait until we graduate. I will leave school and get a job that will support us," WL told Elizabeth.

Vesta was a sizable hurdle for them. She was not convinced that Elizabeth was the best choice for her son. She was wary of their relationship. Others thought she was being overprotective. Elizabeth possessed a strong personality and a great deal of self-confidence. Vesta was similarly domineering and opinionated so there were visible sparks between these two women. In spite of his mother's certain displeasure, WL fearlessly moved forward with his plans to marry Elizabeth. He finished the semester at Maryville College then left for Nashville, seeking employment there. WL had Stuart as an ally—Stuart had moved to Nashville a year earlier and was working as an account auditor at the Andrew Jackson Hotel and encouraged WL to interview for open positions there.

When he finally arrived, WL was thrilled to be in the big city. There was an extra room in Stuart's rental house, so WL had a place to stay. The brothers were happy to be together again after a couple of years apart. The opportunity to work at the same location was also exciting for them. The plan was that Stuart would take WL to the hotel and introduce him to the management, and that WL would be a good fit for one of the open positions.

When he first walked into the newly constructed Andrew Jackson Hotel, he was dazzled by the beautiful decor, modern conveniences, and luxurious atmosphere. Though his upbringing was considered upper class in his hometown, this was a whole new level of the kind of luxury lifestyle he wanted to live and provide for his future family. What better place to learn and observe as well as meet people who could offer future opportunities? He couldn't wait to tell Elizabeth all about it and share his plans and dreams with her.

Andrew Jackson Hotel

There was a job opening for a hotel steward. He interviewed and was hired on the spot. His duties and responsibilities would require him to provide superior customer service. WL was tall and handsome, with a charming personality, making him the perfect choice for the position. He assisted guests who were checking in and out of the hotel and had oversight of the details for banquets and special events. After his training was completed and he had a weekend to travel home, he took the train to Athens to see his girlfriend and family.

When his train arrived in Athens, WL was welcomed by his sister Marie who picked him up at the station. "How is my favorite sister?" he asked. She laughed and the two began to catch up on life and times. It was nice to hear all about Marie's life activities and not be bogged down with legal details about their father's death. Though they spoke of how much they still missed their father, there was a lighter feeling to their lives now. The train had arrived late, so they decided to turn in and sleep and catch up more in the morning.

WL slept restlessly and only a few hours. He was too excited to see Elizabeth. He had confirmed with Marie that he could borrow her car to drive to Maryville to visit her. When he woke up the next morning, he called her to let her know that he would be at her house soon to see her. They didn't have specific plans, but he had a few things in mind.

Vesta had breakfast ready for him when he came downstairs. She had not seen WL in a few months, and she wasn't going to let him leave before she spent time with him. She was very interested in hearing about his new job at the hotel.

"Are you enjoying your job, WL?" Vesta asked with a burning curiosity.

"Yes, I'm very satisfied with my duties," he replied. "With everything, really."

"I bet it's a big change," Vesta offered, smiling.

"It was a bit of getting used to at first! Ladies in their fancy dresses and fur coats and men in their tuxedos are a common sight in the hotel lobby," he continued. "I have organized several parties and events that were a tremendous success. The Capital building's right by the hotel so we host luncheons for all kinds of government officials, lawyers, and their clients. You could say I am staying busy and working hard, but I like it. And the money is good." Vesta hung on his every word. She was very pleased with his level of job responsibilities but had some concerns. And of course, she couldn't hold in her motherly advice. "The love of money is the root of all evil," she reminded him as she quoted a Bible verse. "Don't get caught up in the perils of the wealthy," she said. Vesta was a deeply religious woman and desired a strong faith in her children.

WL nodded respectfully and offered a thanks for the reminder, but truthfully, he resented her words. Why should he care about what the Bible said when his father was ruthlessly murdered and taken from him? He had resented God for many years but pretended to be a believer, if only to fit in with everyone around him and to avoid conflict. He knew that he was different in his heart, but he kept it to himself.

He turned his focus to the real reason for his visit. He hugged and kissed his mother goodbye as he set out to see Elizabeth. He sensed the hurt and coldness in Vesta's voice as she said goodbye and wished him safe travel, but he didn't care that she disapproved. He was going to make his own choices for his future. He gathered a few items in case they had time for a picnic. It was a beautiful September day. He loaded up the car and drove down Kinser Hill to see his love.

Elizabeth had the biggest smile on her face when she saw him. They ran towards each other with open arms. WL picked her up and kissed her and he spun her around and around, just like he'd seen in the movies. Three months was way too long to be apart. While he'd been working in Nashville, she had spent the summer helping on her parents' farm. The family farm, which boasted a sizeable five hundred acres, was where her father raised and sold mules, horses and cattle. The large orchards kept the whole family busy gathering whatever fruit was in season.

Elizabeth had four younger brothers who helped farm the land as well. Her summer had been busy, but she was now occupied with her first week of her second year of college.

After their initial greeting, WL blurted out, "Let's get married today!"

Elizabeth was visibly shocked at the suggestion, but WL could also see that she was intrigued. "How can we marry today when you live in Nashville and I am in college in Maryville?" she asked.

WL had thought about this many times during the past months. "You can come visit me on your school breaks," he suggested.

"Oh, but my parents and your mother will be so upset!" she exclaimed. She understood that he was asking her to secretly elope. She didn't want to hurt her parents, but also knew that Vesta would have difficulty accepting her, no matter what the timing. Her parents were fond of WL, but she was their only daughter and she knew they would want to be involved in her marriage plans. This unexpected proposal was both delightful and unnerving.

"I don't want to wait any longer," WL said, hearing the passion resonate in his voice. "I want to hold you in my arms all night long and love you forever!"

Elizabeth was overcome by his declaration of love for her and she agreed to marry him that day. They found a minister in nearby Madisonville who was available to officiate that Saturday afternoon. They privately exchanged vows in his study at the church.

WL and Elizabeth were married on September 8th of 1928. He was twenty and she was nineteen. They kept it a secret for ten months before it was announced in the local newspaper.

SHE KEPT SECRET

Mrs. Wesley L. Kinser,
Formerly Miss Elizabeth Russell, daughter
of Mr. and Mrs. A. M. Russell, of Cleveland, whose marriage, Sept. 8, 1928, has
just been announced. The wedding took
place in Madisonville, the Rev. Mr. Kennedy
officiating. Mrs. Kinser is a junior at
Maryville college.

Newspaper Announcement of the Marriage of WL and Elizabeth

The young couple was very much in love. They stayed true to their promise of being together on Elizabeth's school breaks, and the two spent New Year's Eve together. Elizabeth traveled down to Nashville to be with him. WL had the weekend off and reserved a beautiful room for them to enjoy the holiday festivities. This was a belated honeymoon celebration as well. Elizabeth wore a new dress and WL donned his best suit. There was live music and dancing, along with gourmet dinners. These two felt very grown up in such a high-society environment. As the countdown for the New Year began, they looked into one another's eyes with adoration. When the new year rang in, they embraced and kissed. Life was grand and the future was bright.

They documented their weekend getaway by taking photographs atop the hotel roof. The only person in the family who knew of their elopement was Stuart. He was the rooftop photographer when Elizabeth came to town. He was not only a great brother to WL, but a faithful friend and confidant.

Dec. 31, 1928

Photos were taken celebrating New Year's Eve at the Andrew Jackson Hotel with the refection of the famous sign behind them.

Elizabeth had to get back to her college courses and returned to Maryville after their celebration. It was always hard to leave each other, but they looked forward to her returning again on Valentine's Day. WL continued to work and save money for their future. He felt that a better future for his family would be in Nashville. Times were growing tougher and tougher, with the Great Depression sweeping across the nation. He felt blessed to be employed and earning a steady income. It was important to Elizabeth to continue her studies and WL was supportive of her goals. Elizabeth's parents were currently facing business difficulties, so it was important to be near her home to assist her parents.

As planned, Elizabeth joined WL on Valentine's Day for a romantic weekend together at the hotel. Once again, they enjoyed the special menus and musical entertainment provided for all the couples. They were elated to see each other again and celebrated the weekend wholeheartedly. Though it was a heavy burden on both of them keeping their marriage a secret, they found solace in their plan to reveal their marriage to the family after Elizabeth's school semester ended.

Valentine's Day Weekend Celebration

WL and Elizabeth Start a Family

everal months after the announcement of their marriage, WL and Elizabeth learned they were expecting their first child. They couldn't have been happier and relished in discussing their hopes and dreams for their children. WL continued his employment with the Andrew Jackson Hotel and Elizabeth took a faculty job at Calhoun Junior high. She lived with her parents during her pregnancy.

Having good jobs and retaining them was very important to WL and Elizabeth as the Great Depression caused an economic crisis. They decided to keep their current employment, even though it meant they were temporarily living apart. Times had become difficult for Elizabeth's parents, Arthur and Retta Russell. Sadly, they struggled financially and lost their farm to bankruptcy. Throughout the 1920s, farmers battled with low prices on crops and livestock, but Arthur's five hundred acres of farmland had continued to provide a livelihood for his family. During the Depression, out of the kindness and goodness of his heart, he tried to help neighboring farmers stay afloat by taking over notes on their struggling farms. Unfortunately, his generosity hurt his business and he lost everything. The Russell's moved to Cleveland, Tennessee, about thirty minutes away from Calhoun, and opened up a boarding house as a source of income.

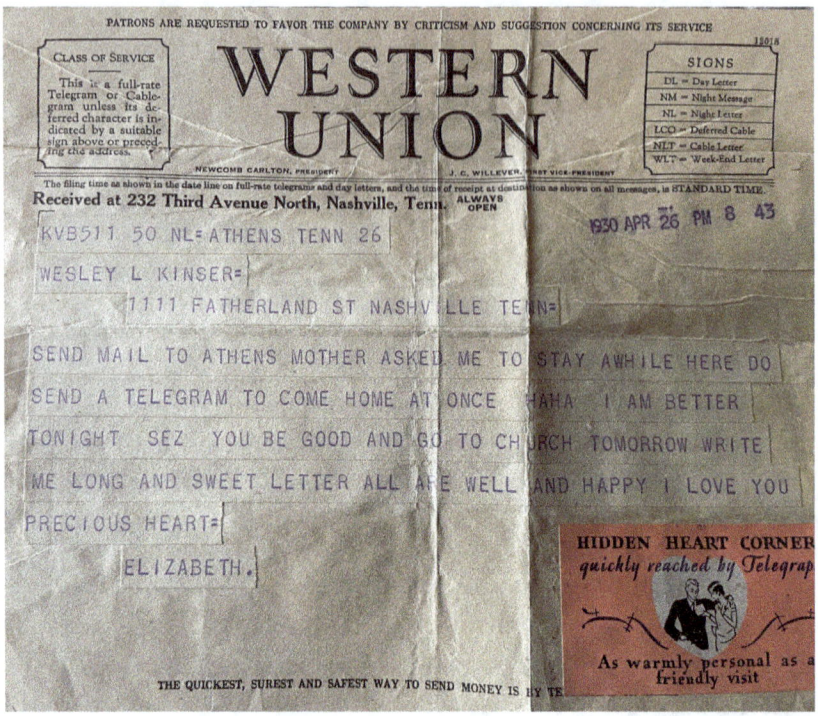

Elizabeth would occasionally send telegrams to WL with special message. In the message depicted above, she wanted him to know that she was feeling better from her morning sickness.

On October 6, 1930, Beverly Ann Kinser was born. She was a beautiful baby with a head full of brown hair. Everyone said she looked just like her father. WL and Elizabeth were such proud new parents, and Vesta, Arthur and Retta were thrilled to be grandparents. WL took time off from work to help Elizabeth after the birth. Marie was also very helpful when they needed anything. WL was sad to leave when he needed to get back to work, but he felt comfortable that his wife and baby were in a safe place. His family was nearby to help her. Elizabeth had to terminate her job at the school, but she didn't mind so much because she had a beautiful baby girl to look at and love.

Since Beverly was the first grandchild on both sides, everyone in the family wanted to see her at any opportunity possible. She was so fun and so happy—a joy to the whole family. In the spring of 1932, she learned that she was going to be a big sister! This was exciting news for everyone.

The merriment of parenthood, however, was abruptly interrupted with some gut-wrenching news. Arthur had not been feeling well. His doctor examined him and the diagnosis was stomach cancer. The family was devastated. Elizabeth truly hoped and prayed that he would live long enough to meet her new baby. She did her best to help her mother care for her younger brother, Merle, who was only eight-years-old when his father was diagnosed. Robert, age twenty-one, and George, nineteen, were establishing themselves in business in the Cleveland area, and Billy was in college. The family appreciated WL because he would come home for family visits as often as possible to encourage Arthur during this difficult time.

After dinner each evening, the Russell family would gather in the living room and listen to *Amos and Andy* or the Sherlock Holmes shows on the radio. Everyone fought to lighten the sad atmosphere surrounding Arthur's illness, and an occasional laugh was welcomed and necessary. The older siblings were very focused on Merle and his well-being, since he was so young. They were a close-knit family and held a deep affection for one another.

Arthur Russell died on April 21st of 1932. Because his father in law was nearing the end, WL came into town that weekend, and was at Arthur's bedside when he passed. Though he was glad to be by his father in law's side during his passing, his emotional reaction was very strong, and he was deeply affected. Such a sad event dredged up the deep-seated loss he had suffered when losing his own father. Arthur had treated WL like a son, so WL felt as though he had lost a father for a second time. The tremendous amount of emotional pain that he had kept bottled up inside of him threatened to give way. He tried to focus on being supportive to his wife as well as her mother to manage his pain. He understood their loss of a husband and father was even greater than his, simply because it was so fresh.

Arthur had been told a few days before his passing that Elizabeth was pregnant with her second child. He smiled broadly upon hearing the news, his face filling with warmth. He was only fifty-seven at the time of his death and died having seen so many admirable accomplishments through in his lifetime. The family rallied around Retta, giving her extra attention and care during her period of grieving. She was forty-nine when she became a widow. Having her granddaughter Beverly at her home was a true solace. She was such a happy baby, and so loving. Beverly's companionship helped ease the pain of such a great loss.

Happy days at the farmhouse of the Russell family when Elizabeth, age 5, is holding the reigns while Bill and George go for a ride.

Elizabeth, Robert, George & Bill

A. M. RUSSELL

Mr. A. M. Russell, whose broad acres lie two miles northwest of Calhoun, is one of the most successful farmers in McMinn County. He ascribes his success to uptodate methods and constant, intelligent and persistent effort. He is a strong believer in intense farming methods and thinks a man is wasting his time unless he makes land produce the very best crop of which it is capable. He owns 500 acres of land in his own right and is interested in some 250 acres more. Every acre that is being farmed is being brought up to the top limit of production. Mr. Russell has discovered that herein lies the secret of the greatest returns upon the investment and labor. Mr. Russell is an extensive raiser and dealer in mules, horses and cattle and always has a good bunch of the best grades and breeds on the farm. In this as in his farming methods Mr. Russell finds the most money in proper care and attention to the best breeds.

Residence and Family Group

Mr. Russell is also developing and proving another fact, and that is that this locality is a good fruit producing section if proper attention is given to variety, planting and care. *These features are found necessary in any fruit country. It requires constant attention, cultivation, spraying, etc. to get best results ... ards any-*

Mr. Russell's especial pride is a 40 acre Alberta Peach orchard that cannot be excelled anywhere. Several car loads were marketed this year and the highest market prices were obtained. He is also developing an apple orchard that promises equally as well, now having 10 acres of bearing trees. Mr. Russell is convinced that all that is necessary to raise fruit here is the right kind of attention. He expects to increase his acreage as fast as possible. Mr. and Mrs. Russell were married some eight years ago, and they have three bright children. A picture of the house and ... together with the apple orchard and a loaded Elberta peach tree are shown on this page.

Apple Orchard

This farm has been greatly improved since Mr. Russell took hold of it and additional improvements are being added each year.

Mr. Russell in addition to his faith in the fruit producing qualities of the soil hereabouts is of the opinion that this is the greatest live stock country on earth if the farmers go at it right.

He finds that in growing the necessary feed and grasses for live stock the land is enriched and made better rather than impoverished by the production of many kinds of crops that the average farm produces year after year.

Elberta Peaches

Mr. Russell produced one of the finest fields of pea hay this year ever found in this valley, and we regret our inability to show a picture of it on this page.

What the Russell brothers have done, and are doing in this County, can be done by others, if willing to put forth the same amount of effort and perseverence.

This is a splendid example of what men who really try can do--easily.

A full-page newspaper article about Arthur Russell and his successful farm.

First formal photo with new baby Wesley

Wesley Luther Kinser, III, was born on December 21st of 1932, in Athens, Tennessee. Such a challenging year had ended in true joy. WL and Elizabeth had been blessed with a son. He weighed in at ten pounds and everyone was amazed that such a small woman as Elizabeth could give birth to such a big baby. Beverly was overjoyed that she had a baby brother and she wouldn't stop giving him kisses. The Kinser family now boasted four members and everything seemed complete.

WL, Elizabeth, Beverly, and Wesley attend church.

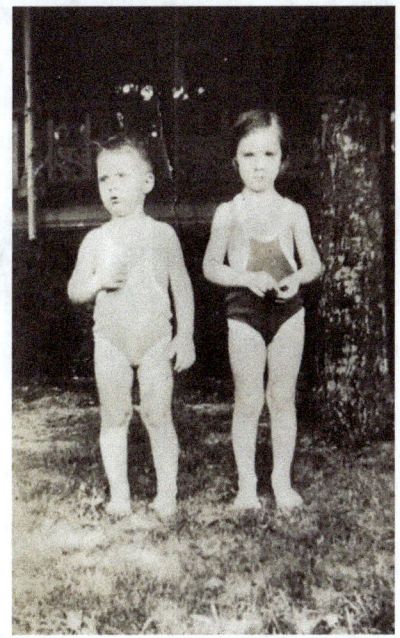

Growing children who love to play and are great friends.

Elizabeth bought a Father's Day Card for the children to give to WL.

Lots of love
   to the finest Dad
Anybody ever had —
Lots of wishes
      happy too
I am glad to send
      to You

Beverly Ann &
Wesley Kinne

Beverly and Wesley forced to stop for a photo,
interrupting their play in the park!

Nashville and WW II

WL and Elizabeth moved from East Tennessee to Nashville to build a future for their growing family. Since WL had been working in the capital city, he felt like Nashville provided great opportunity. They purchased their first home at 2607 Acklen Ave.

2607- Acklen Ave.

Photo from 1938 of the Kinser's newly purchased home.

They were so thrilled to be able to purchase their own home. The location was convenient to everywhere they needed to go, and a short drive to WL's work. WL had left his hotel job for better employment at a local-stove manufacturing company. He worked as a metal worker there. A few years later, he took a job with the postal service.

Beverly and Wesley were approaching school age and the home was around the corner and within walking distance from Eakin Elementary School. A nearby park afforded the children a place to play and for them to meet up with other families for games and picnics. They felt so blessed.

Elizabeth was a stay at home mom when the children were young. She was very creative in saving money for the family and was focused on providing a comfortable life for the future. Being the daughter of a farmer, she knew all about growing vegetables and fruit trees, canning preserves, and making homemade jam. That was her specialty. Family and friends also regularly requested that she make her homemade yeast rolls. They were everyone's favorite.

Elizabeth loved spending time with her children, and she put her whole heart into providing an environment that guaranteed they had a happy childhood. She would read and sing with them and nurtured the areas where they were gifted. Beverly had a beautiful singing voice, so she was enrolled in singing lessons and participated in her church choir. Wesley was an outstanding athlete and played sports daily at the park with friends. He participated in sports from every season. No matter what it was they were enjoying, Elizabeth always had a loving eye on her children.

As they grew older and were in elementary school, she decided to look for work outside the home. Eventually, she took work selling insurance when Wesley started first grade.

Wesley Kinser, Jr., and his sister, Beverly Kinser, are being measured by Gene Kittrell for costumes which they will wear in the Christmas parade Thursday night. Kittrell is costume director for the event.

Elizabeth supported community events and allowed Beverly and Wesley to participate in local activities such as the Christmas parade.

World War II had begun in 1939 and WL was called into service. His brief education at the Tennessee Military Institute helped prepare him for a leadership role in his assignment. He was eventually stationed at Camp Claiborne in Louisiana. Basic training and artillery practice was the primary activity at the base. There was a precision-bombing range there as well. He served as a Sergeant and was dedicated to the men he was training and who were under his command. Though he didn't personally see combat in Europe during his assignment, many soldiers at the camp were trained and sent overseas. WL worked with a group of demolition engineers who were trained to use explosives for demolishing bridges or structures used by the enemy.

WL in his Army uniform.

He found it very difficult to leave his family and especially his children. They were both in elementary school at this point, and there were so many of their school activities that he would be missing. Weekend visits would be rare because Camp Claiborne was a twelve-hour driving commute from Nashville.

The pressure on the family and his marriage was heavy. This was not the life he had hoped for or planned. He didn't want his wife working in a business comprised predominantly of men. He didn't want to be away from his children. He wanted to support his family, but he had little control over his circumstances at this moment in time. He knew serving his country was noble, but the cost was greater that he expected.

Rising to the surface again was the anger and resentment that originally began growing inside of him since his father's murder. Memories of pain and heartache started to come to the surface. There had been so many happy years and times had turned dark again for WL. He felt as though he could explode inside at any second, but he was in the Army where absolute self-control and poise was expected and demanded.

A Failing Marriage

Being absent from his family for months at a time and the stress of possible deployment to fight in the war was unnerving for WL. Furthermore, he received news that his brother Stuart was dying of cancer. That information was deeply upsetting, a devastating blow to him. Serving as an army sergeant meant he was expected to keep a stiff upper lip amidst adversity. He had to appear strong and emotionally in control for his comrades, but he was hurting inside. As a result, coming home on weekend furloughs turned into times of lashing out at Elizabeth because he had so much bottled-up anger and seemingly nowhere else to release it. She did her best to take it all in stride.

His most severe behavioral changes coincided with the news of his brother being sick. Stuart had been diagnosed with lung cancer. WL knew that Stuart's time was short, and this affected him terribly. He grew more and more irritable. When he was home, he was very challenging to be around because he was quarrelsome and complaining, frequently yelling at everyone in the family. Beverly and Wesley were so confused and reacted by keeping a distance from their father. They coped with this change in their father by staying away from the house either playing at the park or at a friend's house.

One weekend when WL was home, he was criticizing Elizabeth more than usual. "You look fat," he would say. "Do you just sit around all day and eat? I'm training soldiers—I get up early, go to bed late, and you are home just lazy around!"

She would reply with calm responses, like, "I stay busy getting the children off to school and helping with homework. I do the cooking, cleaning, and managing the room and board for the renters, as well." She knew he was under great pressure at the army base as well as struggling with the emotional weight of Stuart's illness, so she wanted to be understanding and sensitive.

Conflict arose between WL and Elizabeth when she rented out the upstairs bedrooms after he left for Camp Claiborne. She thought they could use the extra income and didn't realize WL would strongly object. In person, he would act friendly when interacting with the renters, but would complain and fuss about them later. He argued that he didn't want renters in the house with his children in the home. "These are fine people," she told him. "It is a soldier and his wife. They are very nice and pay their rent on time. You know my parents earned a nice income from boarders and we could use the extra income," she explained, trying her best to reason with him. He was not agreeable. Elizabeth was currently providing for the family and felt they needed the additional money. This was her solution and she stuck with her plan.

Sometimes, WL would turn to unfounded and irrational accusations. Most damaging, were his claims that implied she was unfaithful to him. He would taunt her with the question, "How is your boyfriend?" He was referring to a college classmate whom Elizabeth had no interest in and no contact with, either. She rolled her eyes at such an absurd accusation. "WL, I've had enough of this ridiculous talk. When would I have time for someone else? Please stop it or just leave."

On one particular afternoon, what she said or how she said it struck a raw nerve with WL. He became enraged. He slapped her, and proceeded to punch her in the face, and the force broke her nose. "What are you doing?" Elizabeth cried out. "Where does all this anger and rage come from, WL? Get out of here and leave me alone! You need help!"

Elizabeth ran out the door to the next-door neighbor's house to protect herself from any more punches. Blood was pouring down her face and she was crying hysterically. Upon seeing the state she was in, the neighbor called the police immediately. When the authorities arrived, they took one look at Elizabeth and handcuffed WL. They took him to the police station. He was charged with domestic assault, but Elizabeth agreed to allow him to enter into a peace bond and return to his army base.

Sadly, Stuart passed away in August of 1943. He was only forty-four years old and his widow, Bertie, was forty-six. WL returned to Tennessee for his brother's funeral. The family gathered in Athens at Cedar Grove Cemetery for the funeral. Stuart was buried alongside his father and infant brother. WL wanted to comfort his mother, Vesta, and sister, Marie. The three of them, arm in arm, with tears running down their checks, stood beside Stuart's grave. They were reminded of the painful burial of their beloved husband and father, Wesley, Sr. Vesta experienced an added heartache as she thought back to the loss of her firstborn child, Arthur.

The family returned to Kinser Hill after the funeral. Generous friends had prepared meals for the family. The dining room table was covered with an abundance of dishes of food, all delivered by neighbors. For the majority of his life, until he moved away, Stuart was a valued resident of Athens. The outpouring of kindness and condolences was a beautiful comfort for the Kinser family. The community knew how difficult it was for Vesta, Marie, and WL to once again suffer the loss of another loved one.

WL was now the only adult man remaining, at least in his immediate family. He was obligated to leave the next day for Camp Claiborne. He felt like a prisoner, being stationed so far away, and his emotions and thoughts were so overwhelming. He wanted to stay longer with his mother and sister to mourn the loss of Stuart with them, but he had to return to Louisiana. The travel from Tennessee to Louisiana was grueling and he dreaded it. He had traveled by train and the journey was long. Travel time, combined with his work obligation, meant he would not be back to Tennessee until Christmas. His only hope was that Elizabeth would allow him in the home and give him a second chance so the family could be together for the Christmas holidays. Anger and frustration continued to build and fester inside him. He was angry at himself and he was angry about his life circumstances, and he felt powerless to do much about them.

Christmas furlough weekend finally arrived, and WL traveled to Nashville that Friday, on Christmas Eve. After being apart for several months, Elizabeth agreed to have him join the family at home and was hoping he would be on his best behavior. He arrived exhausted and the hour was late. Elizabeth welcomed him and told him about her special breakfast menu for Christmas morning. She told him about the gifts she had wrapped for the children to open. "Beverly and Wesley have decorated the Christmas tree and are very excited to see you. They wanted the tree to look extra festive for you," she said. WL showed no interest in her efforts nor the efforts of the children to create a memorable Christmas celebration for him. He was grouchy and ill-tempered, and Elizabeth was so disappointed that he had arrived with such a sour attitude. Seeing a pillow and blanket set out for him on the sofa, he took off his shoes, laid down and fell asleep. Elizabeth was thankful the children were already asleep and didn't have to witness their father's bad mood. She was likewise exhausted, so she went to bed. Despite the rocky start to her reunion with her husband, she hoped for a happy start to Christmas Day.

The family was home alone this year. Fortunately, the renters had traveled home to visit their own families for the holidays, thus alleviating any foreseeable conflict on that end. Everyone got up Christmas morning and celebrated. "Merry Christmas, Daddy!" Beverly and Wesley shouted, running to hug their father. "We missed you so much!" "Merry Christmas to you and happy belated Birthday, Wes!" WL exclaimed as he embraced them. "I'm so glad to see you and be with you!"

Wesley's eleventh birthday, which occurred on the twenty-first of the month, had already passed. Elizabeth had made a big fuss over Wesley. He had opened his presents and enjoyed his favorite cake with ice cream. Whatever the reason or excuse, she enjoyed celebrating her children whenever she could.

For days, Wesley had spoken about how excited he was that his father was coming home and about having a nice time together as a family.

As they spent the morning together opening presents, WL thought of Stuart and all the joyous Christmas days they had spent together growing up on Kinser Hill. He noticed that deep ache in his heart but returned his focus to enjoying his happy children. The day was generally conflict free and positive, in spite of the discord existing between Elizabeth and WL. They both hoped the children didn't notice. The children were unaware ofthe peace bond order issued on WL. Elizabeth tried to protect them from the burden of stress and worry. From the children's point of view, their father was bravely serving in the Army and that was why he had to be away most of the time.

Throughout the day, WL took several walks outside, circling the house like he was looking for something. For one such outside stroll, the next-door neighbor was in his yard. WL and the neighbor had a brief conversation but were soon interrupted by Beverly and Wesley. "It's so cold outside! What are you looking for, Dad?" they asked. They had come outside to join him in the backyard. "Oh, I'm just looking around," he deceitfully answered. No one in the family would have ever guessed what he had on his mind, but he had covertly revealed his plan to the neighbor.

Meanwhile, inside the home, Elizabeth was preparing an atmosphere suitable for the holidays. She set the table beautifully and served the most delicious food. She was a fabulous cook and family gatherings were her favorite. Christmas Day was turning out to be a wonderful family occasion for the four of them. They had opened gifts around the tree, sang some Christmas carols together, and had spent the afternoon calling out of town family members to wish them Merry Christmas.

"Wesley, tell me," WL smiled while asking a question to which he already knew the answer. "What is your favorite Christmas gift?

"My new baseball bat!" Wesley exclaimed with glee. "Can we try it out tomorrow at the park?"

"Sounds like a good plan to me. You'll be hitting home runs for sure with that bat," WL replied encouragingly. After a long day, they all said good night and went to bed.

Before leaving the living room for her bedroom and turning off the lights to sleep, Elizabeth brought up the subject of an insurance conference that was being offered in Atlanta for agents wanting continuing education and certifications.

"I registered for the event," she said, "and I'll be leaving on March 25th, to drive to Atlanta. I've asked Mary to watch the children for me."

Mary was one of the upstairs apartment renters. This infuriated WL. He hated that Elizabeth was driven professionally and determined to earn income for the family. He had always assumed that financially supporting the family was his role. He laid awake, growing increasingly irritated as he thought about her plans to go to Atlanta. Was she lying about a conference?

Was she meeting someone? So many dark and ominous thoughts ran through his mind and he grew angrier by the minute.

Early the next morning, Elizabeth was awakened by the bed moving and she felt something against her head. "What are you doing?" she asked WL as she could see his silhouette next to her. "I'm going to kill you," he replied as he showed her a hand gun and pointed it to her head. "Put that down," she said authoritatively. "You are not going to shoot me! You'll be in prison the rest of your life and never see your children again! Why would you think you could possibly get away with killing me?" He removed the gun from her head and walked out of the room, gathered his belongings, and left the house to head back to Camp Claiborne.

Elizabeth, alarmed at his behavior, was trembling. She rushed to check on the children. They were soundly sleeping. What was happening to WL? He was not the same person she married. She felt embarrassed by what he had done to her. Regretting that she had trusted him enough to let him stay at home for the holidays, she decided to keep the incident to herself. She laid awake and thought back to the poem that her worried mother had penned after she had eloped with WL. "I hope this sparkling gem you wear will never lose its sparkling flare. If so, you'll then have time to think of Mother's earnest prayer."

With so many marital issues at hand, Elizabeth reflected on her hasty decision to marry WL. She had always thought the poem was written due to her mother's hurt feelings about the elopement. Her mother had expressed concerns about their courtship from the beginning, but Elizabeth had not taken the concerns seriously. In the early days of their relationship, they grew so close and had so much fun together. Elizabeth thought she could give him the love he needed to overcome the horrible effect that his father's murder had on him. How did their marriage get to this place? Was there something worse than his father's murder that had happened in his life? Had an entirely separate event crippled him in controlling his anger and impulses?

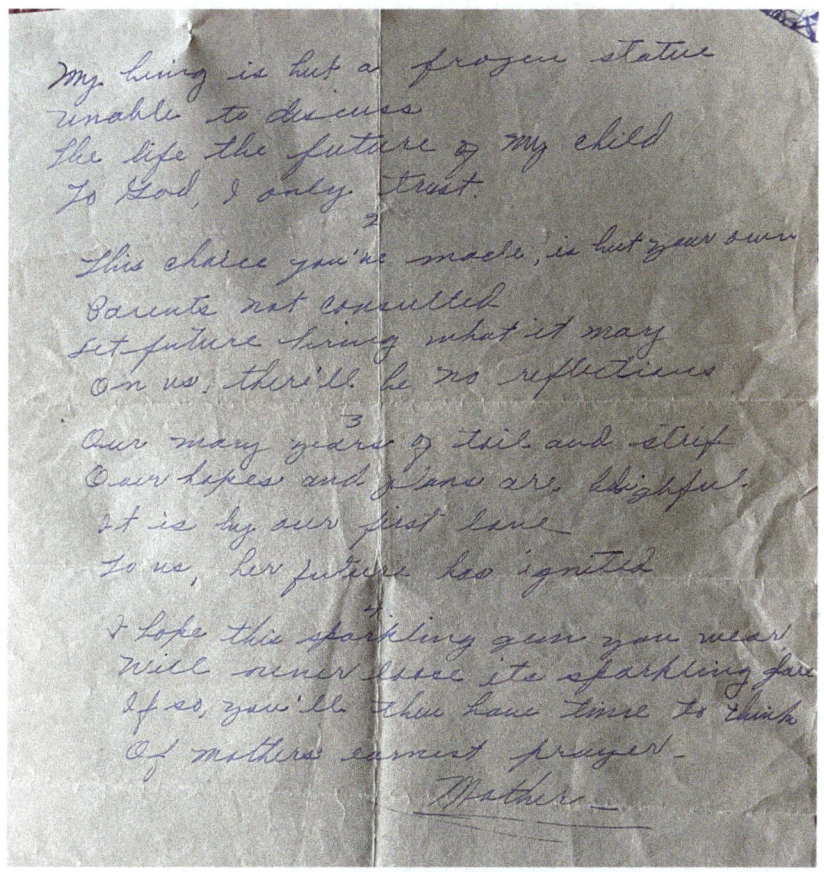

A Poem Written by Elizabeth's Mother, Retta Russell

Elizabeth knew that her wellbeing and the wellbeing of her children was in her hands. She pondered her options, which included going it alone as a single mother if WL didn't change. She wasn't afraid and she loved her children too much to subject them to violence of any kind.

That morning, Beverly and Wesley were looking for their father and he was nowhere to be found. "Mom, Where's Dad?" they asked.

"He was called back to camp," she replied calmly, not wanting to come across upset in any way. "He will be home again soon," she explained in an upbeat tone of voice. "Wesley, your father wants you to practice with your new bat and be ready to play baseball with him when he is home again." She felt so dishonest hiding their father's indiscretions behind his army assignment, but she didn't want them to worry. Beverly and Wesley seemed satisfied enough. They were very proud of the position their father held in the army. They loved seeing him in uniform and viewed him as their strong and brave father keeping our country safe.

Little did they know that their lives were about to be turned upside down.

Attempted Murder

The weekend of March 25th had arrived. Elizabeth said goodbye to the children on Saturday morning then drove to Atlanta to the insurance conference. John and Mary, the couple renting the apartment upstairs agreed to keep an eye on them until she returned. Beverly was a mature and responsible thirteen-year-old and capable of watching over Wesley for the weekend. She was able to get herself and Wesley prepared for school on Monday as well. The two children were very fond of each other and cooperative. Beverly had acquired some cooking skills from her mother, so she easily put together a meal for her brother and herself. They finished up their homework on Saturday morning and Wesley went to play ball with the neighborhood boys. Beverly met up with some friends at the nearby park.

On Sunday evening the telephone rang and Beverly answered. "Hi, Mother!" she chimed happily. "Yes, we had a great day and are ready for school tomorrow." Elizabeth wanted her children to know that she had arrived in Atlanta safely and asked Beverly to pass on that information to John and Mary. "Sure, Mother, and have a great conference. We'll see you in a couple of days," Beverly reassuringly replied.

Not long after Beverly hung up with her mother, her father surprisingly walked into the house.

"Dad, what are you doing here?" Wesley asked.

"I wanted to come see you kids," he told his children. "I had a weekend furlough."

"It is so nice to see you, Dad!" said Beverly.

They chatted for a bit about school activities and classes. Beverly talked about her upcoming choir performances. Wesley informed him that the baseball season was about to begin and eagerly answered all of his father's questions. They enjoyed catching up, but it was getting late. "We have school early tomorrow morning so we should get to bed," Beverly said, as they hugged their dad goodnight.

"Sleep well," he told them. "I'll see you kids in the morning."

WL was home but not with good intentions. He had been thinking through his plan for weeks. He had all the necessary items required. He just needed the time and focus to carry out his plan. He went out to his car to get his bag. He hadn't wanted to bring it inside earlier. He didn't want to risk the children looking inside and seeing what was in his bag. His current role as a sergeant had him overseeing men working as demolition engineers. Over several weeks, he had been collecting dynamite, dynamite caps, fuses, and items needed to make explosives. He confiscated a few items at a time and hid them in his bunk, knowing that no one would suspect a well-respected sergeant. The time for his plan had finally arrived—he was going to destroy his house.

He walked outside and climbed the outdoor stairs up to the separate apartment where the renters lived above them. He was still angry about Elizabeth allowing them to stay in the home. He knocked on the door and the husband answered. "You need to leave now," WL demanded. "I've never wanted you living here, and I definitely don't want you here now."

"What about the children? "John asked. "Elizabeth asked Mary to watch over them while she is away."

"I can take care of my children just fine," WL snapped back.

"Alright, please give us a minute to gather our things and we will leave," John said.

"You have ten minutes to get out or there will be trouble," WL threatened, then walked downstairs and entered his front door.

"WL is in town and wants us out of the house in ten minutes," John said to Mary. "Let's grab our clothes and get out of here. You know how he punched Elizabeth in the face a few months ago. I don't want him to hurt us. He looked angry and he doesn't want our help with his children"

They called some friends to ask if they could stay the night with them. "It's an emergency. I'll explain the situation when I arrive," John told his friend. They got their things together, got in their car and drove away. They could see WL looking out the window as they pulled off.

That evening, while he waited for the children to fall asleep, WL sat down and picked up the Sunday newspaper to pass the time. He read about war news and articles about the local men and women who were involved in voluntary services assisting the war efforts. A thought crossed his mind as he pondered his impending plans. Would his name be in the newspaper this week? Will his plot be discovered? He quickly dismissed the thought. It didn't matter, and he didn't care. His heart felt cold and indifferent. He thought about how he loved his children and knew they loved him. He knew they loved their mother, as well, but he was going to prioritize himself right now. He was discontented with his life and his marriage, and was willing to take drastic measures to alleviate this enormous strain that he felt was crushing him.

Once he knew the children were sleeping, he chose two places to wire his booby traps. Both were used daily by Elizabeth. He started with the iron, which she used daily. It was very important to her that clothes were clean and pressed. She's always about appearances, he bitterly thought. He worked for about two hours to build his first bomb. His other choice was the floor lamp. That one took about three hours to construct. He knew it would be the first light she would turn on when she returned home Monday evening from the conference. His hope was that the light would be the first to explode. The iron was a backup in case the lamp failed. He completed his plan in the early morning hours then fell asleep on the couch.

When he woke up, he gathered his things and wrote a note warning his upstairs renters not to enter the home because there were explosives inside that might detonate. He woke up Beverly and told her to pack a few things and that they needed to leave quickly.

"What's wrong?" she asked.

"I'll explain later," he replied, leaving her to pack.

He woke up Wesley and told him the same thing. "What about school?" the boy asked, rubbing his eyes groggily.

"You'll be missing school today," WL told him, careful to keep any emotion out of his voice. "Hurry, we need to go."

Beverly and Wesley were frightened so they heeded their father's instructions. They grabbed a few of their essential belongings and ran out of the house to the car. Last minute, WL put the warning note on the rail of the stairways going up to the apartment and the three drove off.

"Where are we going?" they asked.

"We're driving to Camp Claiborne, their dad said gruffly. "I need to get back and you are going with me."

"Dad, you are scaring us," Beverly said but no more questions were asked. The children just sat quietly in fear and uncertainty as the car raced down the road. They knew they had a long drive ahead of them. Everything was confusing and unsettling for them. They had seen their dad angry before but this irritated look in their father's eyes was unfamiliar. Yesterday, they had been pleasantly surprised to see him and now, suddenly, they felt like they were in danger.

Meanwhile, a neighbor walking by the house noticed the note by the door and read it. The neighbor was very alarmed and called the police. This was the same neighbor that had spoken with WL during the Christmas holiday. WL had commented to him that his house would be in ashes before long. The comment had seemed strange and out of context in their conversation, so the neighbor just thought he had misunderstood. When he saw the note, he remembered WL's words and it all made sense now.

The police arrived and roped off the house, allowing no one inside. Initially, there was the question as to whether or not it was a hoax. The neighbor told police that WL was stationed at Camp Claiborne. The police called the base and learned that he was due in by that evening. The neighborhood was in a state of frenzy, but no contact could be made with WL until he arrived at Camp Claiborne.

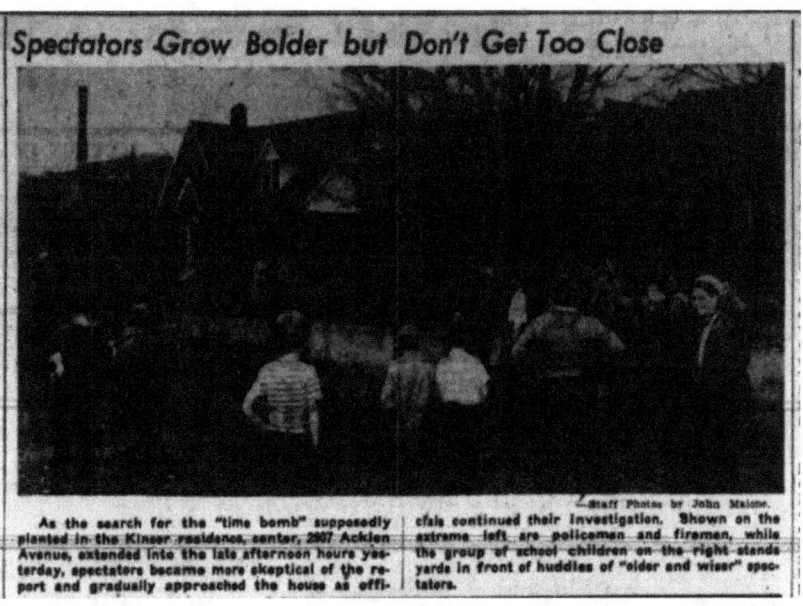

Spectators Grow Bolder but Don't Get Too Close

As the search for the "time bomb" supposedly planted in the Kinser residence, center, 2907 Acklen Avenue, extended into the late afternoon hours yesterday, spectators became more skeptical of the report and gradually approached the house as officials continued their investigation. Shown on the extreme left are policemen and firemen, while the group of school children on the right stands yards in front of huddles of "older and wiser" spectators.

A newspaper photo of the Kinser home with a curious crowd of neighbors gathered to see why the fireman and policemen were surrounding the house.

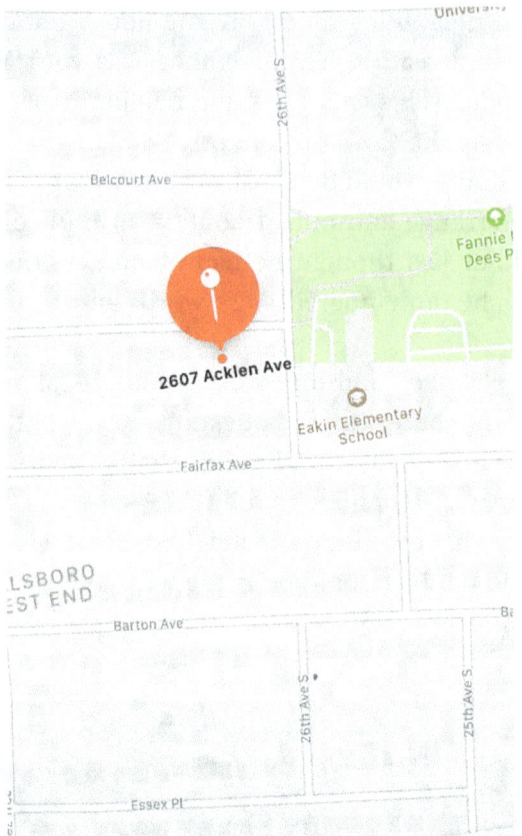

Eakin Elementary School's proximity to 2607 Acklen Avenue

The surrounding neighborhood, as well as Eakin Elementary school, was evacuated when the police learned of the explosives. There was a nine-year-old girl named Carol Ann Tidwell that was picked up at school by her father, Paul. "What is going on, Daddy?" she asked as they got into the car.

"Someone has explosives nearby. The area is being cleared so that no one is in danger," he replied.

Carol Ann's mother, Doye, was still at work, so Paul took off the rest of the day to stay home with his daughter—Carol Ann was their only child and they were naturally protective.

The Tidwell family was familiar with the Kinser family because they lived down the street from Elizabeth's brother, Bill Russell. Carol Ann would play ball with Wesley and the other neighborhood children when Wesley visited his uncle Bill. The Tidwells would learn later that the little boy Wesley Kinser had been put in danger.

The drive to Louisiana took a little longer than usual because WL was so exhausted from being up half the night. Though he was fueled by adrenaline, he did have to stop for a couple of short naps along the way. This was even more disconcerting for Beverly and Wesley. Why was their dad so tired? What had their dad been doing up all night? While he was napping, they would try to comfort each other and stay positive. They didn't know where they were, and they had no way of getting in touch with their mother. They would sit beside each other in the back seat and think of games to play to pass the time. As it grew late and the sky darkened all around them, they felt very anxious about what was ahead. They could no longer see the landscape passing them by as their father drove them south, but they knew they were very far from home.

When they arrived at Camp Claiborne, military authorities were waiting for them at the entrance. Beverly and Wesley took note of their somber faces and rigid posture, and knew something was about to happen that couldn't be good. Their father stepped out of the car and slowly walked towards them. Surrounded by a group of soldiers, their father was taken away by two men who took hold of each arm. He was whisked away quickly, leaving Beverly and Wesley confused and even more afraid.

A kind soldier opened the car door, bent forward and said hello to them. He asked if they were hungry and they nodded. "Your dad has some business to attend to. I'll take you to our service club and get you something to eat."

He walked them over to a building where they had a few choices of food to eat. There were some couches and chairs in the room. They were given blankets and pillows and told to feel free to sleep if they were tired. They were brought some books to read and there was a radio to listen to as well. Some of the men sat around a table talking while they ate and rested. The men were talking very quietly and the children, though they tried, couldn't hear what was being said. They wondered when they would see their dad and find out what was going on.

WL was immediately escorted to the guardhouse, searched and questioned. The search had uncovered T.N.T. and fuses in his pockets in the amount that could have blown up an army barrack.

"Where did you get these explosive materials?" the authorities asked him.

"I acquired them when I worked at the highway department," he replied.

That information was later confirmed as false by family members, because WL had never worked for the highway department. Upon further questioning, he admitted to planting the explosives in his own house but initially wouldn't divulge the whereabouts. He explained that he had planted four setups by wiring them to electrical equipment. Later, he confessed to the electric iron and floor lamp as the only items he set up. After several hours of interrogation, WL was taken to the psychiatric ward and held under observation. Doctors there gave him a battery of tests to determine his mental condition.

Elizabeth returned home to Nashville and was beside herself with worry for her children. She was also in utter despair and disbelief that such an action against her could be devised by her husband of sixteen years. His previous behavior had been shockingly hurtful but how could he attempt such a heinous act?

She called Vesta, her mother-in-law, and reported to her what was happening. She wanted her to know because the event had been published on the front page of the Nashville Tennessean. She didn't want Vesta or the rest of the family to learn about it from someone else, or worse, from the paper itself. Vesta was devastated that her son could concoct such a plan and dare to destroy his wife and endanger his children. The family was in emotional upheaval.

'Bomb' or Pump, It Caused Acklen Avenue Excitement; Spectators Kept Their Distance

By EUGENE FISKE

A "time bomb scare" which excited residents of the Acklen Avenue Natchez Trace section yesterday afternoon was still unsolved last night, with police apparently not yet certain whether the whole thing was a hoax or whether an explosive of some kind was actually hidden in the Acklen Avenue residence of a soldier and his estranged wife.

Huge crowds gathered about the brick bungalow, home of Sgt. and Mrs. W. L. Kinser, Jr., at 2607 Acklen during the afternoon, being held a block or more away by police during the height of

fears the reported bomb was about due to explode, but by dark officers and spectators had left the scene, apparently convinced that no explosion was imminent.

Neighbor Reports Note

The fireworks, minus so far late last night any actual pyrotechnics, started at 10 o'clock yesterday morning when a neighborhood resident reported a note on the dwelling's front porch reporting dangerous explosives set to go off during the afternoon. The officials, aided by a fire engine, rushed to the scene but late last night the nearest clue to a bomb had been the "tick" of a water pump and a refrigerator. Several officers on the scene said they were convinced that the tick-

ing of the basement water pump was the noise that had at first been taken for a bomb, but W. C. O'Lee, divisional highway patrol chief, one of the leaders of the investigation, said that he was still not certain if a bomb might actually have been planted in the house.

State highway patrolmen and city police were stationed at intersections two blocks from the residence on each side during the afternoon until the "deadline" for the explosion passed without bringing a climax, keeping motorists, school children and curious spectators from entering the "danger

(Continued on Page 2, Column 2)

The local newspaper printed its first article about the incident.
The incident was described quite sensationally.

'Bomb' or Pump

(Continued From Page One)

zone." A city fire truck waited nearby.

Experts Make Inspection

First entered by army demolition experts who added action in the South Pacific to their basic training, the house last night had been prowled by numbers of "daring and reckless" investigators who listened intently for the tick of the time bomb expected to blow the neighborhood into oblivion any minute.

Lt. G. H. Hinman of the provost marshal's office here, who first ventured into the "doomed" structure in search of the ticker, said he heard something like a time bomb and was "sure it isn't an alarm clock!"

After hours of periodic hunts through the dwelling for the explosives, a city policeman, half-afraid and half-amused by the "probably unwarranted" excitement, boldly attacked an expensive piano in the living room of the house and "gave with the jive." After several bars of boogie-woogie broke the silence, another group of searchers retired to safety—to be followed later by other erstwhile investigators.

As darkness fell upon the neighborhood, weary officials and residents were still perplexed by the situation, and lingered safely at a distance from the house until the reported danger could be definitely discounted.

Meanwhile, army authorities had wired headquarters at Atlanta, Ga., in an effort to obtain mine-detection equipment for a test of the house.

Quietly investigating the report, Division Chief O'Lee and his men entered the residence before noon and found in a chair near the front door a note which read: "Don't come in here until you see Wesley L. Kinser. Dangerous acid and explosives are stored here."

An alert was immediately broadcast by authorities to "pick up" the army sergeant, but early last night no trace had been found of him. The investigation followed.

Residents Warned

Authorities shortly after noon warned residents of the area to leave their homes until the explosives discharged or could be found and removed. After the "zero hour" residents were told they could return to their dwellings at their own risk, but for another hour or so few seemed to be the "risky" type.

Sergeant and Mrs. Kinser, who have owned the 2607 Acklen Avenue home "six or eight years," have had marital difficulties and been separated periodically for a comparatively long time, neighbors said.

Sergeant Kinser for the past several months has been assigned to an army engineer regiment stationed at Camp Claiborne, La., but returned to Nashville Sunday night on leave, it was learned.

Mrs. Kinser, who has rented two apartments in the house since her husband's induction, left Sunday for Atlanta, Ga., but did not take her two children, 10 and 13-years-old, neighbors told police. The sergeant returned to the residence Sunday night, and left early yesterday taking the children with him.

Couple Ordered Out

"The Kinsers have been having trouble for years. He's been put under a peace bond after beating her up and breaking her nose, and jailed for 10 days for contempt of court in that connection," L. D. Stalcup, 2605 Acklen Avenue, said. "I've heard him threaten to kill his wife and children and burn his home before. He came in last night and told a soldier and his wife occupying one of the apartments to leave, and they left."

Stalcup said Sergeant Kinser resented his wife renting the home, accounting for his attitude toward the renters, and leading to the belief that the "exciting" note may have been left for the benefit of the soldier and his wife.

The army sergeant, Stalcup said, is a former Nashville postal employe who worked for a time as a letter carrier and then in the parcel post department.

Kinser Held, Denies Hoax; Dynamite Search Renewed

Claiborne Soldier May Be Brought Here To Find Explosive; Caps Found at Acklen Avenue Address

Sgt. W. L. Kinser, Jr., who reportedly told military authorities upon his arrest at Camp Claiborne, La., late yesterday afternoon that his note warning persons not to enter his house at 2607 Acklen Avenue for fear of being blown up was "no hoax," may be returned here under guard to enter the house and find dynamite which local officers have been unable to locate.

Maj. John Suther, army provost marshal for the Nashville area, announced last night that he would request Camp Claiborne military authorities this morning to return the soldier "under guard," and bring out the dynamite that 'he has told authorities is in the house."

Major Suther said that after the Monday search of the house for the explosives he telephoned Camp Claiborne authorities and asked them to arrest Kinser upon his return. His call was returned at 7:45 o'clock last night with the news that Kinser had told of how he had fixed the explosives to go off, Major Suther said.

Kinser, now being held in the guard house at the Louisiana camp, had in his possession at the time of his apprehension, Major Suther said, a stick of T. N. T. and some fuses.

Following his statement to the Camp Claiborne authorities, local officers found dynamite caps planted among electric fixtures at the home, but late last night had still not found any dynamite or T. N. T.

Kinser first told military officers, according to Major Suther, that he planted "four setups in the house."

Says Dynamite Planted

He later denied the "four setup" story and confessed that he had planted a fuse to explode two sticks of dynamite in the floor lamp by the piano in the living room and a double amount of dynamite with a fuse in the iron in the kitchen.

Major Suther said Kinser claimed that he had obtained the explosives from "the highway department" where he had worked. Officials, however, were prone to discount the claim since relatives could not recall Kinser's employ-

(Continued on Page 2, Column 4)

Kinser Arrested

(Continued From Page One)

ment with any highway depart
ment.

Meanwhile as half hysterica
residents watched the house las
night, Lt. G. H. Hinman, arm
military police demolition exper
strode cautiously into the structur
and renewed the search for th
dynamite.

The search was renewed afte
Kinser's confession to Camp Clai
borne authorities was relayed t
Major Suther.

Major Suther said last nigh
that he was going to charg
Kinser with "attempted murder'
and that he expected to be subpoenaed to appear in military court
at the Louisiana camp within a few
days.

Hook to Wires Reported

Kinser was quoted as saying he
had "hooked up" the equivalent of
eight sticks of dynamite with wiring in the floor lamp and electric
iron in the house, and these were
the objects of Lieutenant Hinman's
search. Police and army officers
Monday had searched the house
thoroughly when it was reported a
time bomb was set to explode.

With stout rope, Lieutenant Hinman entered the house last night
and wrapped the hemp tightly about
the lamp, eased his way back to the
street, and then ran, pulling the
lamp behind him. When the fix-
ture failed to explode, it was examined carefully by Hinman and
police officials, and a dynamite cap
was discovered hooked to the switch
of the lamp.

The iron was thrown from the
house by Lieutenant Hinman after
he swung it on a piece of rope, and
Patrolman Jim T. Miller tore the
iron open to find another cap as
Kinser had disclosed.

Wiring Disconnected

Prior to entering the house, Tom Byrum, Nashville Electric Service employe, was summoned to the scene and disconnected all electrical wiring leading into the house in order to reduce the amount of danger involved in the search.

Lieutenant Hinman was at Pearl Harbor during the first attack there and, although wounded in the legs, managed to shoot down four Japanese planes during the assault. He went about his work with cool deliberation.

If Kinser's story is true, the house was, in itself, a large bomb, ready to explode at the moment anyone turned on the floor lamp or the iron, authorities said. It was for this reason—although full danger of the situation was not readily seen Monday—that authorities refused to allow any of the apartment residents to remain in the house Monday night.

Children With Him

Sergeant Kinser's note was discovered after he left the house Monday morning with his two children, 10 and 13 years old, neighbors said. The sergeant was serving in Camp Claiborne with a group of demolition engineers. He left early Monday morning with the children, and authorities said the children were with him when he arrived in Camp Claiborne yesterday.

Relatives of Mrs. Kinser said last night that she was remaining in Atlanta for a few days and that the children were receiving care at the Camp Claiborne Service Club and would not return to Nashville for a few days.

Kinser Civil Trial Sought by Officials

A formal request for custody of Sgt. W. L. Kinser, Jr., who was said to have admitted planting dynamite in his home at 2607 Acklen Avenue, will be filed with army authorities by Dist. Atty.-Gen. J. Carlton Loser, it was announced yesterday.

Loser said he has conferred with W. C. O'Lee, division chief, state highway patrol, State Fire Marshall Kirk Webb and Maj. John Suther, provost marshal of the Nashville area, and that it has been agreed to attempt to bring the soldier here to face civil trial on charges of attempted first degree murder.

The trio of police, fire and military authorities returned to Nashville yesterday. They said the army is conducting an investigation of the matter at Camp Claiborne, La., and refused to deliver Kinser into their custody for return here. However, Camp Claiborne officials suggested that the formal request be filed, they said.

Kinser, who is undergoing mental examination at the camp hospital, insisted, the investigators said, that the dynamite caps found in a lamp and an electric iron at his home Tuesday night were the only explosives he planted in the residence.

Numerous articles were published in the newspaper throughout the following weeks, giving updates on the case. This was a very dark time in the lives of WL's family members. The family had been through a tremendous tragedy and now they were facing unbelievable troubles.

Two Mothers in Anguish

Vesta Kinser got up early the next morning after hearing the sobering news about her youngest son. It was absolutely awful to try and fit it all in her head. She walked down Kinser Hill and over to the cemetery where she had recently buried her dear Stuart. Tears were streaming down her face as she arrived at the graveyard. Her heart ached every time she entered the cemetery gates. She had many loved ones buried at Cedar Grove Cemetery.

Beside her husband, was the headstone of her infant son Arthur that she never got to watch grow up. It was still a bitter and hard truth, that she never got to hear the sound of his voice or to feel his arms around her as she planted a kiss on his cheek. There was the headstone of her beloved husband Wesley, who was cruelly and heartlessly taken from her. He would have known what to do in such a crisis. More importantly, WL would not have experienced such a life-altering tragedy if the evil man had not pulled the trigger. He would have had his father to raise him to be a man of virtue. Perhaps what was happening now in his life, would not be happening.

Finally, there was the freshly dug grave of her son Stuart. It had only been six months since his passing and the winter months had not allowed the grass to grow over the dirt. Her heart ached as her eyes scanned the resting place of her love ones.

As she stood at her husband's grave, she asked him, "What have I done wrong, to deserve this? How did our son develop such a black heart? What can I do for him?" Although she knew audible words would not return to her, she felt some comfort just being in his presence. The word 'pray' looped in her thoughts over and over. She knew that prayer was the only viable offering she had in this situation. "I miss you so much. I miss you every day, every hour and every minute. Please keep watching over me and being my strength as I continue to press forward in this crazy world."

She walked over to Stuart's grave, and spoke audibly as tears ran down her cheeks. "I could have never managed without you, my dearest Stuart. Thank you for being the most wonderful son to me, and the truest big brother that a boy and man could have. You stood by your brother's side when your father was murdered. You sacrificed your plans and future for him. You provided opportunities for him that he would not have initiated himself. Thank you, sweet Stuart. I miss you more than you will ever know. You have been my rock. You have been Marie's rock. Our hearts feel so empty without you."

Vesta returned home and called Elizabeth. This was a time that these two women could put aside their differences as they were united in concern and anguish over their loved ones. Vesta was equally worried for Beverly and Wesley, and was eager to help with them in any way she could, though she lived a three-hour drive away from Nashville. Elizabeth told her that she had just arranged for the children to take a train home and she would pick them up that evening. They were being escorted by a Camp Claiborne soldier who was also traveling to Nashville. Elizabeth was staying at her brother's house while the investigation was continuing in her home. "Vesta, I'll let you know as soon as the children arrive," Elizabeth said.

As the week's events unfolded, the Nashville newspaper covered the details of the event. The reporters were writing about it for several consecutive days now. It was a horrible embarrassment to Elizabeth, and she wanted to do anything possible to protect her children. She secured a lawyer because she knew the marriage was over. She knew that staying with WL any longer was impossible after he had tried to kill her and had endangered the children. Her anger was not exclusive of the public spectacle that had been brought on them all. Broken-hearted and in perpetual disbelief, she filed for divorce. WL's trial was ahead of her. Staying strong for her children was her top priority.

As soon as Vesta was able to speak to her son, she took the opportunity. She had several days of contemplation over what to say. WL called her from jail.

As soon as she said hello, WL broke down crying. "I am so sorry, Mother. I lost my head and now I've lost my family. I have had so much anger growing inside me and I should have gotten help long before now. Please forgive me, Mother," he pleaded.

"Son, I will always love you. And I forgive you too," replied Vesta.

The two discussed the psychiatric help he was getting at the base. He told her that, for the first time in his life he was able to talk in depth about his deep-seated and buried anger, along with the resentment regarding his father's murder.

"When Stuart died, I just felt like I was going to explode inside," he explained. "I lost my father and now I've lost my brother and best friend. While I've been detained here, I've been looking back at everything. I realize that I just felt so trapped. I felt like I couldn't breathe. I just wanted out of my pain and my life. My actions towards Elizabeth were deplorable. I've handled this so badly. I'm thirty-five years old and I have ruined my life!" WL could barely speak from weeping.

Vesta listened attentively and confirmed her love for him. "Please, let the doctors help you deal with your anger. That's all I ask of you," Vesta urged him, and with that, they said goodbye.

Beverly and Wesley arrived in Nashville and Elizabeth profusely thanked the young soldier for keeping an eye on them. She hugged her children so tightly and asked, "Are you both okay?" Before they could answer she said, "I'm so sorry I wasn't in town. I won't ever leave you again. I'm so sorry that you've had to go through this. I promise this will never happen again!"

"We're fine mother," Beverly exclaimed, and Wesley agreed. "What happened? What did Daddy do?" they both asked, almost simultaneously. No one had yet filled them in, and their father had not hurt them, so though they knew he was in some kind of trouble, they did not know what it could possibly be. Their faces were full of questions.

Elizabeth attempted to explain to her children what their father had done without upsetting them too much. She knew the information in the newspaper articles could be repeated to them at school, and even twisted disproportionally, so she had to tell them everything that was written, as well as what was true and what wasn't. She described their father as being ill and explained to them that this was why he did what he did. She didn't want to hurt their tender hearts because she knew they loved their father. She reassured them that their father loved them very much and his actions did not lessen his love for them. Defining the situation was one of the toughest things she had ever done in her life.

For the time being, Elizabeth and her children stayed with her brother Bill. She was near enough her home that she could get information and updates about the explosives from the police. Eventually, all danger was removed. The children were able to return to school and regular activities. The house had undergone a thorough search and just needed to be restored to its original state. Everything from cabinets to bed mattresses had been torn apart in the ongoing search that had taken place in her home. When the investigation was over, she was able to return home and attempt to establish a normal life again for her children. Beverly and Wesley were treated with kindness and respect at school. Neither teachers nor classmates mentioned the recent events or newspaper articles. The school principal spoke with Beverly and Wesley before returning to class, telling them, "If you need anything, don't hesitate to ask me. If anyone bothers you about what happened with your father, let me know immediately and I will call them into my office." That gave Beverly and Wesley comfort because they, too, felt embarrassed by their father's actions towards their mother.

Vesta continued to check in on Elizabeth and ask how the children were doing. Elizabeth informed Vesta that she was filing for divorce and kept her mother-in-law informed on the criminal proceedings against him. Though Vesta was cordial and seemingly understanding, Elizabeth knew their already strained relationship would be very limited in the future. She had no intention of letting her young children be involved with their father. She would never allow them to be in any type of danger. She didn't know what the outcome of the trial would be, but she would protect her children at any cost.

Trial and Punishment

formal charge of attempted first-degree murder was filed against WL and he was subpoenaed to face a civil trial in Nashville. It was originally determined that he would face a general court-martial, but the army authorities decided to return him under guard to Nashville for civilian prosecution. After several days of observation and being examined by the army medical team, he was declared to be mentally stable and released to be incarcerated in Nashville.

Though his future was uncertain as far as his freedom to the outside world, his future was very clear as to his relationships with his wife and children. Those relationships were severed. His children would be adults before he would know if they would ever interact again. This initially created an unfortunate rift and divide between Elizabeth and her children's grandmother, Vesta Kinser, and their Aunt Marie. Elizabeth was bound and determined to protect her children and immediately after this incident she trusted no one in the Kinser family.

When the court date arrived there was much anxiety on the part of WL and Elizabeth. The estrangement between the two was strong. Elizabeth had developed even more indignation as the weeks passed. She knew she was now alone when it came to financially providing for Beverly and Wesley because WL would be in prison. She was under a huge burden but knew there was no alternative. She entered the courtroom with her head held high and a staunch mindset as the proceedings began.

"All rise," called the bailiff as the judge walked into court. Elizabeth stood up looking straight ahead. She and her lawyer were ready with their testimony for the judge.

WL stood with his lawyer and he looked over at Elizabeth. The time he sat in jail had softened his heart and he felt remorse for his actions. He was truly hoping that she would have mercy on him and that the charge against him would be lightened. Being the first time they had been in the same room since she left for her conference, Elizabeth had no desire to exchange any words with WL. She felt so hurt and angry. How could the man she loved so much attempt to kill her and try to kill her so cruelly? She had spent several weeks pondering that surreal question.

As the charges were discussed and each lawyer presented their case, the judge listened intently.

For Elizabeth's attorney it was cut and dry. He simply recounted the facts of the matter. "There is no denying that Sergeant Kinser wired explosives to the floor lamp and an electric iron in an attempt to kill or at the least harm his wife," he said.

Elizabeth was asked to describe her impressions of the situation and share her thoughts and wishes. "My children were taken from their home without my permission, and they travelled in a car for hours to a place where they knew no one. Then their father was taken away from them and was clearly in trouble and, at the time, they did not know why." Elizabeth explained what had happened with great passion in her voice. "I do not want them to ever have such an experience again! Now they must live with the knowledge that their father tried to kill their mother." She continued to express her desire to protect them from any such future outbursts or indiscretions.

WL's attorney had a more psychological approach to his defense. He asked the judge to consider the trauma that WL experienced as a boy. He presented documents from the psychological evaluations and described latent pain and despair over the murder of his father that led to such dysfunctional actions. His attorney pointed out that WL had not received any grief counseling as a teenage boy and the tragedy was suppressed. The death of his brother Stuart was also raised as a contributing factor in his abominable actions. "Stuart was his brother, father figure and best friend since he was thirteen years old. The impact of this recent loss only six months ago cannot be overlooked," his lawyer stressed.

The mental anguish every soldier was facing with the current challenges of WWII was also presented as a defense point. WL was working with demolition engineers. He described the use of explosives as a somewhat normal and daily thought process because he worked with them and trained his soldiers how to assemble and detonate. He also argued that the explosives actually never detonated so, in essence, it wasn't his desire or intention to kill his wife but just threaten. WL's attorney stated, "My client admits that his actions of setting up explosives in the house was an outrageous act, but he only meant to frighten, and not to kill or harm anyone. He knew how to construct explosives, but they were not properly assembled or they would have exploded. The fact that he left a note on the door as a warning shows his intention was only to frighten and threaten but not to kill. My client is guilty of a stupid act but fortunately no one was harmed."

The judge called for a recess and called Elizabeth and her attorney into his chambers. Mrs. Kinser," he began. "I will do whatever you want in this case. I know your greatest concern is your children and I want to offer you another option based on some of your stated concerns. I can either lock up Mr. Kinser for the rest of his life or I can send him back to the army base and he can stay under the army's control. What do you prefer?"

Elizabeth consulted with her lawyer then gave the judge her decision. "I would rather have WL in the army instead of placing the stigma of an incarcerated father upon my children."

"So it will be," replied the judge.

Upon returning to the courtroom, the judge issued his ruling as WL stood nervously beside his attorney. "Mr. Kinser, I have never had a case like this. Your actions are appalling, and you deserve to be locked up in our prison system for a long time. You are very fortunate that the woman you married and who is the mother of your children has more character and love for her children than you could ever begin to comprehend. Mrs. Kinser has asked that, instead of incarceration, you be returned to Camp Claiborne and continue your counseling and therapy. She has agreed to a long-term assignment to an army life in lieu of prison. You are not to contact her, but you are allowed to write your children letters that she will pass on to them at her discretion. I hope you understand the leniency you are receiving with this ruling." The judge paused as he waited for a response from WL.

"Thank you, Your Honor," WL replied. "And thank you, Elizabeth. I truly appreciate this second chance."

The court was dismissed and the bailiff escorted WL to his current cell until he could be transported back to Camp Claiborne. There was no exchange of words or glances between WL and Elizabeth as he was led away. Elizabeth and her lawyer exited the courtroom and further discussed the matter of her divorce. She was soon to be released from her marriage and free to start her life over again. She had high hopes of a happy and productive life for herself, Beverly and Wesley from this day forward. This chapter of her life was about to end.

A Single Mother Recovers

As a single mother, Elizabeth was determined to succeed. She continued with her room-and-board income from renters in the rooms on her upstairs floor. She had emotional support from her brother Bill and sister-in-law, Virginia, who lived nearby. Bill had developed a career in home building. Elizabeth decided upon a career in real estate and sold Bill's newly-built homes. They were a good brother and sister team.

As she pursued her real estate career, she was in turn pursued by a very kind and handsome man named Hugh Lokey. Hugh had been a highway patrolman but had left that field to become a realtor.

Working as agents for Marvin G. Hall and Company is where they met and began their partnership selling homes. Eventually, they opened their own business and named it Lokey-Kinser Realty Company and a formal announcement was made on February 6th, 1949.

Elizabeth was one of the first women brokers in Nashville.

Elizabeth was once again happily married and hopeful for her future. Elizabeth sold her home on Acklen Avenue and the Lokeys bought a home on four acres located on Elysian Fields Road, also in Nashville. It was a lovely and spacious home that was perfect for entertaining family and friends. Imitating Elizabeth's upbringing, they planted an orchard of apple and peach trees and a garden of all types of vegetables. This was her dream home, and a fresh start for her, and she couldn't have been happier.

Lokey-Kinser Vows Are Said

Mrs. A. M. Russell announces the marriage of her daughter, Mrs. Elizabeth Russell Kinser, to Hugh G. Lokey, son of the late Mr. and Mrs. B. C. Lokey.

The ceremony took place Oct. 28 at Belmont Methodist church with Dr. E. P. Anderson officiating. Immediately after the ceremony R. L. Russell, brother of the bride, entertained at a dinner at Hundred Oaks after which the couple left for a southern bridal trip.

Mr. and Mrs. Lokey are making their home on Elysian Fields road and are both connected with Lokey and Kinser Realty Co.

Every Sunday, the Nashville Tennessean newspaper included a section advertising homes listed by Lokey-Kinser. Hugh and Elizabeth were a dynamic real estate duo and their business was thriving. They were thrilled. They had an office in downtown

Nashville on Union Street, but were also able to work from home. The flexibility in their schedule was perfect, enabling them to spend time attending performances or games of the children. Beverly was a student at Belmont College and Wesley was a senior in high school and soon to be a college freshman playing football at Maryville College.

Once he was off to school and no longer living at home, there were weekends when Hugh and Elizabeth would drive to Maryville to visit Wesley. Accompanying them each time was Wesley's girlfriend, Carol Ann.

Hugh enjoyed working in the garden just as much as Elizabeth loved it. The afternoon of November 25th, they were both home, preparing for the Thanksgiving Day celebration. Wesley was coming home from Maryville the next day, Beverly's fiancé Charlie was in town, and Elizabeth was cooking for the extended family. She was in the kitchen working on her menu and Hugh decided to take a walk outside to enjoy a break in the rain that day. The temperature was a pleasant sixty degrees and colder weather was predicted for Thanksgiving Day.

He had not felt well for several days and he thought a peaceful walk in the yard would be helpful. Business had been so demanding and he was looking forward to a little rest and relaxation. "Elizabeth, I'm going to take a walk outside since it stopped drizzling. I'll be back in a few minutes," he called out to her. "Alright, enjoy your walk," she replied, as she continued to focus on her holiday menu.

Though busy in the kitchen, Elizabeth noticed that Hugh had been gone an unusually long time. It was beginning to get dark and she began to wonder where he could have gone. She put down her cooking utensils and walked over to the breakfast room window to look outside to see what he was doing. She saw him lying on the ground. In a panic, she ran outside calling his name, "Hugh, Hugh are you okay?"

He did not reply, and he did not move. When she reached him, she lightly shook him, calling his name. She checked to see if he was breathing. He was not breathing. Hugh was dead. Elizabeth called an ambulance immediately. When the paramedics arrived, they pronounced Hugh dead at 5:30 pm. She learned later that he died of a cerebral hemorrhage. He was only forty-eight years old.

idnesdsy Morning, Nov. 26, 1952 **19**

Hugh G. Lokey Dies at Home

Funeral Arrangements Incomplete for Member Of Real Estate Firm

Hugh G. Lokey
Former highway patrolman

Hugh G. Lokey, 48, Nashville real estate man and former state highway patrolman, died at 5:30 p.m. yesterday at his home, 786 Elysian Field road, after suffering a cerebral hemorrhage.

Elizabeth was devastated once again. Hugh had helped her overcome the sadness of her past and the brightness of her future had finally been shining upon her. They had recently celebrated their second anniversary of marriage. Now, she was forced to bury her husband of only two years. She was alone again. Business had been very good, so she wasn't under too much pressure financially. She would once again be supporting herself and now Wesley, who was in college. Elizabeth grieved Hugh's death throughout the holiday season and as the new year began.

The Children Thrive

Beverly and Wesley found their way very productively throughout their high school and college years. The trauma and distress of their early life passed, though the memories remained. Beverly found her talents in studies and music. Wesley found his strengths to be in athletics. Their mother was so proud of their accomplishments. Sadly, their father missed out on his children's activities and events other than to hear about them through letters they wrote to him.

Beverly was a beautiful young woman who not only was an excellent student but had a lovely singing voice. She was active in school and church choir, as well as working hard in her school subjects. She participated in sorority socials and dances and was a member and treasurer of the Epsilon Beta chapter of the Nu Phi Mu sorority. After Christmas of her Sophomore year, the sorority members entertained at a Silver Star Ball at The Rawlings banquet hall. Beverly wore a beautiful gown and her date was a friend from her birthplace of Athens, Tennessee. Beverly's beauty and personality attracted attention from boys at other schools. She was invited to attend a dinner dance at the elite Belle Meade Country Club with a boy from a local boys' school.

Beverly was a member of the stage crew at West High's drama club and graduated from West High School in 1948. She went on to study at Belmont College and was a member of the first graduating class being recognized at the commencement as achieving honors and awards.

Value of 'Eternal Verities' Cited at Belmont

—Staff Photo by Bob White

Members of Belmont College's first graduating class, who received certificates and awards at the commencemnet program in the college auditorium today are, from left, front row: Theta Bara Overton of Bethpage, Tenn., Margaret Anne Robey, Barbara Ann Redden, Betty Anne Brintle of Cornersville, Tenn., and Beverly Ann Kinser; back row, Emma Jane LeFevre, John W. O'Rear, William T. Malone, Carl R. Martin and Mary Louise Prentiss of Montgomery, Ala.

Beverly graduated with honors from Belmont College in 1952.

Belmont Graduates Hear Dr. Hill on Freedoms

Emphasis must be placed on this country's principles of political and religious freedom, unparalleled material resources and faith if we are to have a victorious tomorrow during these times of confusion.

This statement was made yesterday by Dr. John L. Hill, promotion director for Baptist assemblies at Ridgecrest, N. C., and Gorieta, N. M., during graduation services at Belmont Baptist college.

Faith Strongest Verity

Without integrity, life is a failure regardless of what things one may possess, he continued. "Faith is possibly the strongest of all verities—in God, in the future and in tificate in piano and a diploma in voice.

Associate in Arts

Receiving the title of associate in arts were William Troy Malone and Carl Reynolds Martin, both of Nashville, and Theta Bara Overton of Bethpage, Tenn.

The awards were presented by Dr. Warren F. Jones, acting Belmont president and also president of Union university, Jackson, Tenn.

Delivering the invocation and benediction were Dr. Harold J. Purdy, pastor of Belmont Heights Baptist church, and the Rev. Don J. Pinson of Eastland Baptist church.

ourselves and our own convictions," Dr. Hill declared.

Following the principal address, certificates were presented to 10 seniors, the college's first graduating students.

Receive Certificates

Receiving certificates of accomplishment were:

John William O'Rear, Beverly Ann Kinser and Margaret Anne Robey, all of Nashville, Betty Ann Brintle of Cornersville, Emma Jane LeFevre and Barbara Ann Redden, both of Old Hickory.

Mary Louise Prentiss of Montgomery, Ala., was presented a cer-

Despite the tragic loss that Elizabeth had suffered with the passing of her husband, she had her daughter's achievements to brighten her days. Beverly's accomplishments didn't end with college. It was then that, soon after graduation, she was engaged to a dashing young man named Charlie. He was from South Carolina and worked at Dupont.

Her Engagement Is of Interest

—Photo by Loveman's

Mrs. Elizabeth K. Lokey announces the engagement of her daughter, Miss Beverly Ann Kinser to Charles Randall Quattlebaum. The wedding will take place Jan. 31.

There was an especially bright spot on the horizon for Elizabeth, and that was the upcoming wedding of her daughter, which was planned for January 31st of the following year. Elizabeth turned her focus to celebrating Beverly, and all the while her heart was healing from such a crushing blow.

Beverly's upcoming marriage was highly celebrated!

Miss Kinser To Be Honored

In honor of Miss Beverly Ann Kinser, whose marriage of Charles Randall Quattlebaum, of Leesville, S. C. will take place Jan. 31, Mrs. Carl Anderson, Mrs. Ernest White and Mrs. W. L. Little will entertain at a tea this afternoon. The affair will be given at the home of the bride-elect's mother, Mrs. Elizabeth Kinser Lokey, at 786 Elysian Fields road.

Arrangements of white stock and roses will be used to decorate throughout the reception rooms. Approximately 150 guests will call between 2 and 4 o'clock. An arrangement of the chosen blossoms will also be used as the central ornament for the serving table.

Completing the decoration of the board will be white tapers burning in silver candelabra.

Assisting in the hospitality will be Miss Carol Ann Tidwell, who will keep the guest register, Miss Geneva Wade and Miss Dorothy Wilson and Miss Frances Isabel, who will preside at the tea table. Miss Ann Stark, pianist, will present a program of music throughout the afternoon.

Taking place at the home of her parents on Elysian Fields road was the marriage of Miss Beverly Ann Kinser and Charles Randall Quattlebaum. The bride is a daughter of Mrs. Elizabeth Kinser Lokey.

Quattlebaum-Kinser Vows Said at Home Ceremony

At a beautifully planned home ceremony yesterday afternoon Miss Beverly Ann Kinser, daughter of Mrs. Elizabeth Kinser Lokey, became the bride of Charles Randall Quattlebaum, son of Mr. and Mrs. George C. Quattlebaum of Leesville, S. C.

The home of the bride's mother, 786 Elysian Fields road was the scene of the wedding at 4 o'clock, at which the officiant was Dr. G. Allen West, pastor of Woodmont Baptist church. A musical Barbara Feldkircher, Miss Molly Anderson and Miss Carol Ann Tidwell.

Mr. and Mrs. Quattlebaum of Leesville, parents of the bridegroom, assisted in receiving.

After the reception, Mr. Quattlebaum and his bride left for a short wedding trip. After Feb. 5, they will be at home in Leesville.

Guests from a distance here for the wedding were Mr. and Mrs. Robert Shealy, Carroll Cockrill, and Gerald Quattlebaum, all of Leesville; and Earl Copeland of Athens, Tenn.

program was presented by Mrs. Robert B. Baker, pianist and Dee Wayne White, vocalist.

The ceremony took place before the fireplace in the living room. On the mantel was an arrangement of white roses combined with string smilax, and throughout the reception rooms were decorative arrangements of other white flowers.

The bride entered with her brother, Wesley L. Kinser III. by whom she was given in marriage. She wore an early spring costume suit of imported ciel blue flannel, the collar and pockets of which were finished with beaded embroidery. With the suit were worn a white blouse, navy accessories, and a close-fitted white velour hat covered with pearls, rhinestones, and bugle beads. On the white Bible carried by the bride was an arrangement of white orchids and lilies of the valley.

Miss Dorothy Wilson of Old Hickory was the bride's only attendant, wearing a dressmaker suit of navy blue, a navy hat, and matching accessories. Her flowers were pink roses in a hand bouquet.

Hamilton Kiser of Leesville, S. C., was Mr. Quattlebaum's best man.

After the ceremony, Mrs. Lokey, mother of the bride, entertained at a wedding reception. Refreshments were served from a table in the dining room covered by a lace cloth, having a decorated wedding cake at one end. In the center of the table was an arrangement of white roses and smilax. Assisting in serving were Miss Helen Brandon, Miss Joyce Standley, Miss

Details of the Newlyweds Nuptials.

Elizabeth, Wesley, Beverly, Charlie and his parents on the wedding day.

Charlie and Beverly moved to South Carolina and began their new lives together and started their family. They had three lovely and gifted children, Kathy, Randall, and Russell, who were the joy of their parents' lives.

Russell, Randall, Charlie, Beverly, and Kathy circa 1965

Wesley Falls in Love
with Carol Ann

After the attempted murder of his mother, Wesley spent a lot of time at his Uncle Bill and Aunt Virginia Russell's house on Capers Ave. Elizabeth and the children lived there several weeks. The family home was undergoing a full police search and afterwards needed to be put back in order. The Tidwell family, who were neighbors and lived a few houses down the street, knew and befriended the Russell family and met the Kinser family. Carol Ann Tidwell often joined in playing ball with Wesley and his younger cousins, Billy and Buddy. She would hold Wesley's baby cousin, Melba, and swing her on the porch swing. Their families were very sociable towards each other. Wesley was two years ahead of Carol Ann in school and he developed a crush on her at a very early age. He always found a way to visit his aunt and uncle with secret hopes of seeing Carol Ann at the same time.

Doye, Carol Ann and Paul Tidwell

Carol Ann's family were hardworking and kind, and people who knew them considered them upstanding, decent people. No family tragedy or criminal activity existed in their past. Carol Ann's father, Paul Tidwell, was a sales manager as well as part owner and distributor of Pabst Blue Ribbon Beer in Nashville.

He and his company were very active in community events and sports team sponsorships.

—staff photo by Jimmy Ellis

Ellis Cook, left, of Beer Distributing Co., presents a check for co-sponsorship of e Capital City Golf Association Open tournament slated this week at McCabe. om left with Cook are J. B. Blanks of the CCGA, Beer Distributing executive Paul dwell, and CCGA president Dick Saunders.

Paul and his coworkers, supporting a citywide event.

Doye, donning her hospital uniform dress, was thrilled
with her employment at Vanderbilt Hospital

Carol Ann's mother, Doye, worked at Vanderbilt Hospital and organized the schedules for all the resident doctors at the hospital. As a young girl, Doye wanted to be a nurse but her father was against it and refused to let her go to nursing school. Because she was a very talented pianist, his dream for her was that she teach music. Though she did teach piano for a few years, after marrying Paul she followed her heart in nursing. Her significant position at Vanderbilt was a satisfying replacement for teaching piano.

Carol Ann was an only child and very close to her mother's side of the family. Her grandparents, Lily and Silas, lived nearby, as did her Uncle Carlton, Aunt Eddy and older cousin Maxine. They gathered often for celebrations of birthdays and holidays.

Her Uncle Howard and Aunt Mildred lived in New Orleans with her younger cousin, Tommy. She would travel to visit them every summer break and grew very close to her Aunt Mildred. Although she was sad when Mildred and Howard divorced, she was happy that Mildred moved back to Nashville so she could see her more often.

Tommy moved to Dallas and went to college at SMU. Music talent was strong in the family. Tommy, who later went by his given name of Howard, became a Dallas high school music teacher and band director. His high school marching bands were award-winning. He could play almost every instrument used in a marching band and he would travel during the summer months and hold band camps. One year, he visited Lipscomb University and all of his Nashville relatives were able to see him conduct at the camp concert. His family was so proud of his success. His ultimate achievement was co-founding the Dallas Wind Symphony.

Mildred and Howard "Tommy" Dunn

One of several albums recorded when Howard was the conductor
and artistic director of the Dallas Wind Symphony

Sandlot Doings

Richland Park outslugged Elizabeth Park 13 to 10 in a softball tussle at Elizabeth Park yesterday. The Richland nine will tangle with Park Avenue next Tuesday.

Wesley Kinser pitched a no-hit game as Calvert trounced South park 11 to 0 in a softball tussle at South park yesterday.

Wesley Pitched a No-Hit Game!

Though Wesley did not have a father figure at home to encourage his involvement in sports, he started his sports career early. He especially loved baseball and excelled.

Wesley was a Junior at West High School when Carol Ann started her freshman year. He was a star athlete, and Carol Ann couldn't help but notice him and find herself reciprocating a romantic interest in him. When they saw each other in the hallways between classes, they would stop and talk for a short minute, catching up on how the day was going for each other. Sometimes, they exchanged little notes so they could touch hands for a second or two. The feelings grew throughout the school year. When she became a sophomore, and Wesley was in his senior year, they started dating exclusively. She was a cheerleader and he was the quarterback of the West High football team. He was extra inspired to play his best game with his cherished girlfriend cheering him on. After the games, they would go to a local restaurant called Varellos with friends, and eat French fries and drink Coca Cola.

Carol Ann's curfew of 11:30pm was strictly enforced by her parents. The only exception was when there were sorority dances. There was a large group of sorority girls and their dates who would go out together after the dance. They would stay out until the early morning hours and end their dates by getting breakfast at a local diner. The Tidwell's trusted Wesley and knew their daughter was safe and well protected in his company.

Carol Ann ready to cheer for her boyfriend

Quarterback Wesley ready to win the game and impress his girlfriend

Wesley created a strong bond with the family by joining in their favorite leisure activities at home. Paul set up croquet and badminton in his backyard and the four of them would spend the afternoon together playing those games. Though Wesley had wonderful uncles nearby, it was refreshing for him to feel part of a close-knit family with a man like Paul Tidwell, who was such a positive role model for him.

Lovebirds

Wesley graduated high school and moved to East Tennessee to attend Maryville College, where he played on the football, basketball and baseball teams. It was Elizabeth that insisted he attend Maryville College, as it was her alma mater. He really didn't want to leave Carol Ann behind, but playing sports in college was a great opportunity. "I'm going to miss you so much. I love you and will be thinking about you every minute of every day. Every week I will write and call," he told her. Wesley was definitely a hopeless romantic.

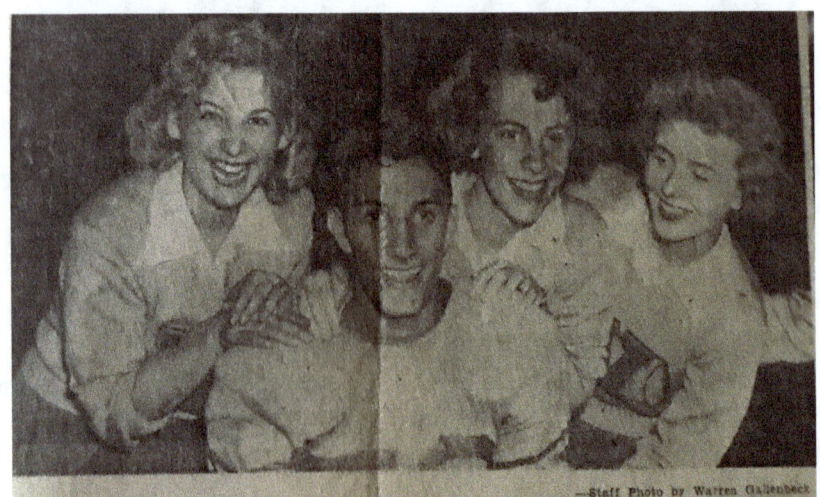

—Staff Photo by Warren Gallenbeck

BLUES HERO—A trio of pretty West High cheerleaders surround Joel Berlin in the fading minutes of last night's 19-6 upset of traditional rival East. Berlin passed for two touchdowns and engineered the Jays' victory with his slick ball-handling. The cheerleaders (from left) Sonia Kantor, Ja... Smith and Carol Ann Tidwell.

Carol Ann on the far right with West High Cheering Squad.

Carol Ann continued cheerleading her junior and senior years of high school. Wesley kept his promise to call and write, and after two years away in Maryville, he could no longer bear the physical distance between them, and returned to Nashville to be near his true love. He transferred to Vanderbilt University and played on the baseball team. At one point, he held the school record for the longest distance on a home run hit.

BANNER, Tues., April 22, 1952

—Photo by Vic Cooley

REUNION—Former West High and Larry Gilbert Junior League teammates, Jimmy Patterson (left) and Wesley Kinser, hold a reunion following Maryville College's 4-2 victory over Lipscomb College yesterday on the Bison's diamond. Patterson hurled brilliantly for Lipscomb in defeat, permitting only three hits and striking out 15, while Kinser played errorless ball at first base for Maryville.

Wesley pictured with friend who played for the Lipscomb Bisons.

VU Starters Named For Tilt With Miami

By JOHN BIBB

VANDERBILT'S Coach Dave Scobey yesterday named his starting team for the Commodore baseball opener tomorrow at McGugin field against Miami, Ohio, university.

Included in the starting unit are two freshmen, a sophomore, five lettermen and Senior Wesley Kinser who has been the hitting star of the Commodore spring drills.

The frosh starters are Second Baseman Mike Tancill and Centerfielder Gary Page. Tancill is a fancy-fielding youngster from Kirkwood, Mo., and Page is the former Litton high ace who has been outstanding both defensively and offensively in the preseason workouts.

Lettermen in Scobey's lineup are Captain Jimmy Miller, catcher; Pitcher Charlie Hawkins, First Baseman Floyd Teas, Third Baseman Jim Looney and Outfielder Johnny David.

Kinser, a transfer student from Maryville college who finishes Vanderbilt in June, and Sophomore Hollis Johnson, shortstop, round out the Vandy starting lineup.

"There is a good possibility that the lineup might be changed between now and Monday afternoon," Scobey said after yesterday's 10-inning intrasquad game, "but right now those are the men I expect to start."

Among the men sure to continue challenging for starting positions is Outfielder Lee Carlson who led Vandy's hitters last spring with a .377 mark. It will be difficult to keep Carlson on the bench.

Kinser was the hitting hero of yesterday's drill. He hit safely three of four times at bat, clouting a triple, off the windows of the Vandy swimming pool and followed up with a double and a single. They finally got him out on a hefty belt to centerfield.

Tancill also did a good job hitting, picking up three singles in five trips. During the 10 innings he also drew a couple of walks.

Bill Keller, freshman basketball star, took pitching honors in the game. He worked four innings and didn't give up a hit. He had a shaky start, walking two men and hitting another in his first inning. But he settled down and struck out five men.

Miami, also opening its schedule against the Commodores, is expected to arrive this afternoon. The Redskins are on their annual southern tour and following the game with Vanderbilt they have contests scheduled with Middle Tennessee State and Tennessee Tech.

♦ ♦ ♦

Following yesterday's game Scobey announced an 18-man squad, cutting down after the pre-season drills.

The 18 men are:

Pitchers—Bill Keller, Charlie Hawkins, Johnny Bennett, Jim Fleming, Red McDaniel, Wilson Tate.

Catchers—Captain Jimmy Miller, DeWitt Evans.

Infielders—Jim Looney, Melvin Smith, Floyd Teas, Hollis Johnson, Mike Tancill, Jerry Caldwell.

Outfielders—Lee Carlson, Johnny David, Wesley Kinser, Gary Page.

Wesley was named as a Vanderbilt starter in the 1952 season and commended for his hitting skills. In this newspaper article, he was described as "the hitting star" and "the hitting hero."

—Staff photo by Jack Corn

Vanderbilt's baseball team will go after its fourth SEC triumph playing Kentucky here this afternoon. The Commodores won their third conference game by stopping Kentucky, 9-0 yesterday. Front row from left are Johnny David, Lee Carlson, Gary Page, Johnny Bennett, Captain Jimmy Miller, Melvin Smith, Mike Tancill, Jim Flemming and Red McDaniel. Second row, from left, are Manager Dave Scobey, Hollis Johnson, Floyd Teas, Wilson Tate, Bill Keller, Charles Hawkins, Jerry Caldwell, Wes Kinser, Jim Looney, Dawiss Evans, and Manager David Williams.

Wesley joined Phi Kappa Sigma fraternity at Vanderbilt and developed lifelong friendships. He graduated with a business degree and Elizabeth could not have been happier or prouder. Her dreams for her children had come true. They had triumphed over their troubled upbringing.

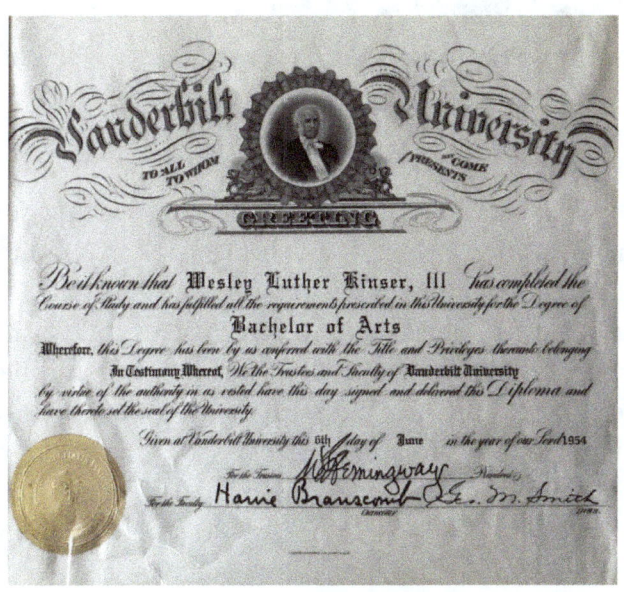

Wesley's Graduation Day

Wesley's most important life event was asking for Carol Ann's hand in marriage and, much to his heart's content, she said yes! Originally, they were to marry in June, but Carol Ann changed her mind. She said she had cold feet and wasn't ready to get married. This change of plans was not received well by Doye. In fact, she was quite unhappy about it because the bridesmaids had been asked, the church was booked and the announcement had gone public. But Paul took on the understanding role, and told his daughter, "It's okay, Carol Ann. If you aren't ready to marry, then don't get married."

There was only a three-month delay. Carol Ann changed her mind again over the summer and they were married in the church chapel with the immediate family in attendance. On September 3, 1954, the two tied the knot and another Kinser family was formed.

THE ROMANCE of Carol Ann Tidwell and Wesley Kinser, whose engagement is announced today, got its start at West End High School when Carol Ann was a pretty sophomore cheerleader and Wesley a senior football, basketball, and baseball player. That was four years ago, and they have been dating ever since.

Carol Ann has been wearing Wesley's Phi Kap pin since last year, and at Christmas, she received a beautiful diamond solitaire set in platinum. They are planning a June wedding with all the trimmings at the West End Church of Christ.

Carol Ann's Engagement Photo

MISS CAROL ANN TIDWELL

Announcement is made today by Mr. and Mrs. Paul Tidwell of the engagement of their daughter, Carol Ann, to Wesley Luther Kinser, III, son of Mrs. Elizabeth Kinser Lokey. Mr. Kinser will be graduated in June from Vanderbilt University.

—Photo by Walden S. Fabry

After a one-week honeymoon in Gatlinburg, Tennessee, Wesley and Carol Ann moved to Elizabethtown, Kentucky, where he began his basic training at Fort Knox army base. After basic training, Wesley was moved to Germany for his overseas tour in the army. He got an apartment and situated in his new role and Carol Ann arrived a few weeks later. They would travel throughout Europe on weekends and made wonderful memories together. Traveling to Paris, the city of love, was their most popular experience. When his tour was over, he returned to Nashville, got his real estate license, and joined his mom in the family business.

This photo was taken on April 17th of 1955, on the harbor at Bremerhaven, Germany. Wesley was twenty-two years old and a newlywed.

Private First Class Wesley Kinser, III walking down the street in Germany.

When Wesley and Carol Ann started their family, they were blessed with three daughters: Julie, Amy, and Lee Ann.

Elizabeth Finds Love and Happiness Again

After the loss of her husband Hugh, Elizabeth continued to work and build her real estate business. Wesley had joined her and the two added other agents and partnered with local builders in Nashville. As time passed and Elizabeth could focus more on her future, she considered the idea of another relationship. Some clients took a special interest in Elizabeth and introduced her to a good friend. He lived in St. Louis but came to Nashville especially to meet Elizabeth. His name was Fred Hoeffler. The two had both lost their spouses years earlier. They really hit it off when they met. They began talking by phone each day and he would come to Nashville for visits. She traveled to St. Louis to visit him as well.

After several months getting to know each other, the two decided to marry. Fred was not far away from retiring from his job, so Elizabeth moved to St. Louis. She got her Missouri real estate license and sold houses in the St. Louis area. They planned on moving back to Nashville after he retired so they could be near family. They resided in St. Louis for a couple of years.

Mrs. Lokey, Mr. Hoeffler Are Married

The marriage of Mrs. Elizabeth Russell Lokey and Fred P. Hoeffler of St. Louis took place at 4 p.m. Saturday in Ferguson Memorial chapel, Belmont Methodist church.

Dr. E. P. Anderson officiated. Wesley L. Kinser III gave his mother in marriage.

Mrs. Charles R. Quattlebaum, daughter of the bride, was matron of honor, and Dr. Dennis F. Hoeffler of St. Louis was best man for his father. Ushers were William P. Russell Jr. and George A. Russell Jr., nephews of the bride.

Following the ceremony, a reception was held at the church.

After a wedding trip to Hawaii, the couple will reside in St. Louis, where Mr. Hoeffler is district operating manager of Graybar Electric Co., Inc.

Elizabeth could not have been happier to have her granddaughters, Julie and Kathy, with her at her wedding.

Elizabeth's grandchildren photographed all together at her home.

Elizabeth enjoyed her new life and growing family for many years to come until her passing on June 24th, 2000, at the age of ninety-one.

Marie Kinser, The Final Resident on Kinser Hill

arie was sixty-three years old when her mother, Vesta, passed away. She remained the only resident in the home and the house was willed to her, along with all items inside of it. Marie was not married, and she had no children. She had a big decision ahead of her as to stay or go. She had cared for her elderly mother and she was now free to live her final days in whatever way she wanted to live them. She had lived on Kinser Hill her whole life. It was all she'd ever known, but there were new possibilities in her future.

Marie was a kind and loving aunt and kept in regular contact with her niece, Beverly, and her nephew, Wesley. Both Beverly and Wesley were born in Athens. By now, Wesley had lived in Nashville for the majority of his life. He would invite Marie into his home and would take his family to visit her in Athens. He had named his oldest daughter, Julie Marie, after his dear Aunt Marie Kinser. It was a loving gesture of appreciation for the wonderful lady that Marie was in his life.

Marie Kinser and her namesake Julie Marie Kinser,
photographed together at her home on Kinser Hill.

There was a widower in town who Marie had been getting to
know. His name was Lee Moses. During WW II, he had served
as a Captain in the 117th Infantry. He was an upstanding and
well-respected gentleman in the community. After the 1946
Battle of Athens ended, Lee was the City Recorder and had been
left with the responsibility of dealing with the battle-scarred
city's affairs. The friendship between Marie and Lee had been
growing strong over the recent years and, after Vesta was laid to
rest, Lee and Marie decided to marry.

Tennessee Wesleyan University was located down the road
from Kinser Hill. The school was growing and wanted to expand
their facilities. Marie decided to sell her property to the school.
They purchased the home and land with the intention to raze
the home and build a baseball field and sports facility. Before
she sold, she held an estate sale in the home to sell items that

she could not use in her new home. Along with many items that she did keep, she took the stairway banister to be installed in the new home that she and Lee bought. For the whole of her life, she had run up and down the stairs holding on to the beautiful wood banister, and it was a memory she wanted to include in her new life.

When the day came to close on the sale of Kinser Hill, Marie walked around the house one last time. A flood of memories washed over her as she walked through each room. She thought of her wonderful childhood and her loving parents. She reminisced about her dear older brother Stuart, who had been her protector and best friend. She thought back to the day her baby brother WL was born and the excitement the family enjoyed together. She thought about the twenty-one years of special family celebrations they shared and took part in before the devastating murder of her father ripped their family apart. Thoughts of the trials and heartache when her father did not receive justice also ran through her mind. It felt surreal to Marie that soon this beautiful Victorian home, where she experienced so many life events, was soon to be torn down. Had she made the right decision? Should she have kept the house and the history there intact? Her emotions were so strong. She walked outside and stood on the porch looking at the land and trees. Many hours of running and playing with friends and family flashed through her mind. She looked up to the sky and prayed, "Thank you, Lord, for the blessed life I have lived on Kinser Hill. Thank you for the memories that I carry with me. Thank you for the new future ahead of me. Bless this place and may it reward many young people in the future." She walked down the porch stairs for a final time.

Marie and Lee married on October 24th, 1964, and were married almost thirteen years until her passing on October 15th, 1977. She served her city as mayoress or some would say First Lady of Athens when Lee was elected Mayor of Athens in 1969. She was a very humble lady and those who knew her described her as lovely and classy. She served as chairman of the Cedar Grove Beautification Committee. What an appropriate position for her, because she had her loved ones resting there. She watched over their resting place with loving care. Spending years as a member of the Athens Chapter 159 Order of the Eternal Star, she ultimately served as Past Matron. She had strong faith in God, was very active in her church and taught Sunday school for many years.

The Kinser family, dear friends, and the city of Athens, Tennessee, lost a jewel of a lady when Marie passed away.

Lee and Marie Kinser Moses outside their home in Athens.
Wesley, Julie and Lee Ann Kinser travelled from Nashville for a visit.
The photographer was Carol Ann Kinser.

Wesley and his three daughters visit Lee and Marie.

Marie and Shaun the Sheep Dog at the Kinser home in Nashville.

What Happened to WL Kinser?

After being sentenced to return to Camp Claiborne as an alternative to prison, WL returned to Louisiana to serve his time. He spent eight months there until the camp was deactivated in 1945, as WW II was coming to an end. He was released with an honorable discharge from the army. He returned to Nashville and was reinstated at his postal job.

One day he knocked on the door of Elizabeth's house on Acklen Ave. She was home and opened the door to an unexpected and shocking surprise. Dressed in a suit and tie, she was not influenced by his handsome appearance and kind voice that once made her heart melt.

"What are you doing here? You are supposed to be in Louisiana," she exclaimed. "The Camp was closed down and I was released," he explained. "I just interviewed for a job and I'll be working at the post office again.""You are not welcome here, WL. Please don't knock on my door again. I will contact the police if you come near me or the children again," Elizabeth warned. She meant every word. She had moved on with her life and was finally experiencing a time of peace for herself and her children. She knew WL would bring nothing but chaos into their lives.

WL knew Elizabeth was serious. He left and didn't come back. While working at the post office his curiosity about what Elizabeth was doing got him into trouble. He was caught mail rifling.

He had opened mail that belonged to Elizabeth and another woman in the area. He was arrested and convicted of mail tampering but later released from jail under $1000 bond. He was fined for his offense and fired from his job. Deciding to get a new start someplace far away, he left Nashville.

Kinser Bound Over To Federal Jury

Wesley J. Kinser, Jr., 201 Twenty-first Avenue, South, was held to the grand jury yesterday on charges of tampering with the mails after he waived a preliminary hearing before U. S. Commissioner Lee Brock.

Kinser, former army sergeant and suspended Nashville post office letter carrier, is accused of removing mail from two letters, one addressed to his estranged wife, who lives at 2607 Acklen Avenue, and another addressed to the wife of a service man in the Murphy addition.

WL moved to Ft Worth, TX and enrolled at Texas Christian University. He studied accounting and began working as a tax consultant. He married twice again in his lifetime, divorced his second wife, and his third wife outlived him. He never had any more children. He attended a local Baptist church and was a member of the Shriners and American Legion. His final years were free of legal problems and he lived trying to better himself as a person. When Beverly and Wesley became adults, more contact was made with their father through phone calls and letters. He visited Wesley and Carol Ann in their first home when they were brand new parents. He spent time with Beverly and her children in later years. He was able to spend extended time with his grandsons Randall and Russell while they were in high school in the mid-1970s. They enjoyed WL sharing his hobby of photography with them as they watched him develop photos in his home studio.

When his sister Marie passed away in October of 1977, he drove to Tennessee for her funeral in Athens. After her funeral, he traveled to Nashville and briefly stopped by his son Wesley's home one evening to discuss Marie's Will and Testament with him. The father and son sat in the family room for a couple of hours reading over Marie's will. His granddaughters were home that evening and were introduced to their grandfather for the first time. Other than saying hello, WL made little effort to speak with them or get to know them. Perhaps the fact that so many years had passed by with no contact or involvement with his granddaughters made the thought of building relationships too daunting a task. To his granddaughters, he was simply a stranger and he chose to keep it that way. At that point in time, his granddaughters were completely unaware of his history with his ex-wife, their grandmother they knew so well and affectionately called Mema. Maybe he made the best choice to stay a stranger.

Meeting his granddaughters could have been a time of celebration. Walking into his son's beautiful home and witnessing his son's success as a father and businessman would have been a perfect time to give praise and congratulations. WL did none of that. Certainly Wesley would have appreciated some commendation. Certainly the granddaughters would have benefited from a warm memory created on that evening. Wesley had very low expectations of his father and sadly those expectations were met. Excuses for WL's behavior could be made—he did not have his father to set an example for him and he didn't seek help from others to learn important relationship skills for building a bond with his own son. As WL stood up to leave, he said goodbye to Wesley and the two men shook hands for the last time.

WL died of a heart attack two years later on November 21, 1979, at the age of seventy-one. He was living in Benbrook, TX, and was buried at Greenwood Cemetery in White Settlement, TX.

Prior to his death, WL was the last living person that had once resided on Kinser Hill. He was the last person to be born on Kinser Hill and he was the youngest person who ever lived on Kinser Hill. In the end, this deeply troubled man outlived all other members of his immediate family that ever lived on Kinser Hill.

Special Extras

Formerly Kinser Hill—Students participate in baseball practice at the Tennessee Wesleyan University. TWU won the NAIA Championship in 2012 and 2019.

TWU Baseball Field

On Elizabeth's eighty-first birthday, Wesley wrote a letter of appreciation to his mother. An insight to the relationship of a mother and son and an example of his tender heart that remained after such a challenging childhood.

August 13, 1990

Dear Mother,

I thought I would write you a letter of appreciation for your 81st Birthday. These expressions are not meant to be words of flattery but sharing with you my appreciation from a sincere heart.

First of all, an expression of gratitude that I had you as a Mother who has loved and taught me, cared for me. You have been the only person in my life who has loved me unconditionally. Who has been a source of dependency, being able to count on you whatever the circumstances or situations. I believe you have inbreeded this kind of love within me, which I share with my children and family.

During times of financial strain you have generously offered to help even when it was a burden to you. You have offered encouragement and motherly advice in times when I have wrestled with problems.

As a 57-year-old, if I am worthy of my salt, I need to be emotionally and financially dependent on myself with a mature independency. Even with your strong motherly instincts, you offered me a freedom of movement and independence when I was recently living with you. This I appreciated because I know it wasn't easy for you to do.

You have a lot of spunk and your will to continue to enjoy life and other people I admire. You continue to have a mind of your own that you freely express. "The cat is Black."

I value being brought up in the Christian faith, taught to work, even the discipline that was inflicted on me. (The little tree switches.) The positive attitude you conveyed that built my self-esteem and self-worth. I remember, when I was about five, the story about the train engine: "I can; I can; I can." How you implanted in my mind I was a leader, could do anything I set my mind to do. How you taught me to spoon my soup, table manners, and etiquette. How you instilled within me the Christian work ethic, to be an achiever, a strong moral and value system. Also, the times you took me on Real Estate appointments and taught me the Real Estate business.

It is hard for a lot of people to understand how I can say and defend that I had a happy childhood when there were many situations, happenings, and problems that occurred. I believe it was your love and dedication that made it possible for me to have a happy childhood. Your undying belief in me and how I wanted to fulfill your belief in me so that you would be proud of me. That has always been important to me.

We all managed and shared the hard times. I appreciate you as a working woman in the business world. How you didn't give up and how others in the profession respect you. I appreciate that you were able to provide the funds to put me through college so that I might have a good education that would benefit me in the business world.

I appreciate that any anger or hurt toward Daddy did not prevent you from keeping intact my relationship with Grandmother Kinser and Marie. They also played a special part in my life, and you encouraged and kept that relationship alive.

I appreciate the fact that when Carol Ann and I got married and I became a part of West End Church of Christ, you did not try to bind me to the Methodist Church. This is something I've only come to recognize and appreciate in recent years. I appreciate your help financially in making it possible for Carol Ann and I to buy our first house at 729 Newberry Rd. I appreciate the financial help ($500 a month) that made it possible for me to take care of my family and go into Real Estate. Your faith in me gave me the opportunity to expand the Real Estate business you started and gave me the start needed to provide more than adequately for my family.

I appreciate your love and affection for my daughters and granddaughters. How you are always in remembrance of them on special occasions, and throughout the year.

When people ask me when is my birthday and I say "December", this comment implies you're so near Christmas your birthday is forgotten. I inform them the opposite is truth. My birthday has always been a great day of celebration, and in a large part I contribute that to you.

There are, of course, many, many more areas of thanks and appreciation for all you've done for me over the years. You have been a wonderful Mother.

If over the years I have failed to show in words or action how meaningful and important you have been to me, I hope this letter will clarify my shortcoming.

I know you have worried and had a motherly concern regarding my life over the past few years. However, I believe many of the problems and situations are nothing more than trials to make me a better man, parent, husband, and son. I'm looking forward to the next 20 years of my life being the happiest and most productive of my life. (God willing) I expect you to be here to enjoy them with me.

Wishing you a HAPPY BIRTHDAY and many more to come with good health, a sharp mind, and a loving heart.

With Love,

When visiting the McMinn County Living Heritage Museum, an employee looked in the storage room to find this photo. The museum archived this once displayed picture of a local woman photographed with the Kinser Hill home behind her.

The Acklen Avenue house, where a crowd of spectators gathered in 1944, is still standing today. This photo was taken in 2019.

This illustration is found on the first page of Marie's memory book. When she glued it to the page she was merely a teenager and unaware how this humorous drawing would be relevant in her future.

About the Author

Julie Kinser Huffman currently resides in Houston, TX, and works as a property manager. Becoming a published author began with a personal story entitled "I Forgive Me" included in the book *Chicken Soup for the Soul: The Power of Forgiveness*.

A proud graduate of the University of Colorado in Boulder, Julie began her college career at Lipscomb University where she was honored to serve as co-captain of LU's inaugural women's basketball team. She has lived overseas in London, England, and Stockholm, Sweden, where she learned to speak Swedish.

Julie Kinser Huffman standing on the former Kinser Hill which is now the location of Tennessee Wesleyan University sports facility and baseball field.

Julie has three children; Viktoria, Lindsay and Stefan. She always says that her children are the greatest blessing and accomplishment of her life.

Final thoughts from the author after writing this book...

My family story contained several shocking surprises for me. My ancestor's lives were messy and riddled with flaws, but I have learned about love, compassion, forgiveness, and bravery from them. My relatives have taught me that though our lives may not turn out as we imagined or planned; perseverance in adversity will bring future blessings. It is important to never give up hope for bettering your future.

I was a toddler when I visited my great grandmother on Kinser Hill. It would have been wonderful to visit the home in my adult years. I am honored to have acquired an antique bookcase that once had its place in the house. It hugs the wall in my family room and I sit next to it when I drink my morning coffee. My imagination carries me back in time envisioning my great grandmother or Aunt Marie enjoying their coffee seated by the bookcase. That would truly be history repeating itself. Meanwhile, I am thrilled knowing that young people are benefited by the sports facilities that were built when the home was removed.

I was asked if I was going to use my family's real names in this book because of the potentially shaming actions of my grandfather, to which I answered yes. In the words of George Bernard Shaw, "If you can't get rid of the family skeleton, you may as well make it dance." Life would be monotonous if there were no dancing skeletons.

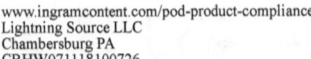